I Was a Stranger

and You Invited Me In

The Story of two Sudanese "Lost Boys" and two Senior Citizens

by Sue Bruscia
with Joseph Kelly and Paul Yana

Published by Bamboo4Sale.com in 2009

Printed in California

Dedication

To Bruce, my beloved husband of 32 years who is a
wonderful leader in our home and a great encourager to
Joseph, Paul and myself. His inspiration and help on
this project meant the world to me! He truly exemplifies
the love of Jesus, our Lord and Savior who has made
this all possible!

Acknowledgments

Without the following people, this project wouldn't have been possible:

- Joseph and Paul for their great courage, input, and incredible vulnerability
- The many friends and family members mentioned in this book and some whose names were not
- The dedicated social workers at Adopt International and Catholic Charities of Santa Clara County
- The many generous foster families who have opened their hearts and homes to those in need
- Debra Leigh, and all of the staff at Pacific Coast Charter School
- The faculty, staff, and students at Monte Vista Christian School
- Our wonderful church family at Green Valley Christian Center, who love and embrace Joseph and Paul
- Wendy Nelson and Natalie Samarippa for their prayers and encouragement
- Karen O'Conner for her help and encouragement
- Our "tech-savy" friend, Larry Gullman for his hard work getting this project completed.

Foreword

I left the dark, dreary room in that Eastern European hotel to meet Marcel, the director of the orphanage. As I stepped out of the car, up she jumped into my arms—an adorable little blonde-haired girl. If I hadn't caught her, surely she would have taken a nose-dive. This was my first "up-close-and-personal" encounter with an orphan child. For some years, my heart had been touched by the plight of orphans in Romania. Finally, I was on Romanian soil preparing to work on an orphanage. The Lord had fulfilled my long-held desire!

How difficult it was to say good-bye at the end of the two-week stay! The children had captured my heart! As the tears flowed when we departed, I knew that I was being called to do something more. That "something more" would be gradually unfolded to me in the next five years—even though I was 56 years old at that time!

My husband, Bruce, and I were "empty nesters" and actually enjoying it. Though we missed our three adult children, there were some advantages. The house stayed clean longer. When the phone rang, it was actually for one of us. The best part was that I didn't have to cook so much. Then there was the freedom to go on short-term mission trips. Bruce was self-employed in the insurance industry. We had "ventured out" about five years prior, to Montevideo, Uruguay, to help construct a girl's dorm at a Bible college there. We were part of the "elastic eighteen" from our church who all went on this mission trip. I really didn't want to go, but I didn't want to be apart from Bruce for two weeks, either. So, I reluctantly tagged along. That experience totally changed my life! Working with wonderful people and having so much fun on a project that would have a lasting impact on the Kingdom of our Lord was truly an amazing experience! From that time on, I jumped at the chance to go on other mission trips. We went to places like Tobago, Mexico, inner city Detroit, San Francisco, Prague, and of course, on this trip to Romania to help build an orphanage home at Caminul Felix. I loved children, and I sure had enjoyed my twenty-plus years of teaching youngsters. Now was my chance!

That trip was the beginning of a new venture for us. We came back with the idea of trying to adopt two older Romanian children. At the ages of 50 (I had "robbed the cradle" when I married Bruce) and 56, we knew that it may be a bit challenging. However, we were in good physical condition, and thankfully had the means to proceed. We found an agency—BAAS (Bay Area Adoption Services) that was great to work with. In the next year, we attended meetings, participated in interviews with a social worker, and accomplished our home study.

Meanwhile, in our subsequent trips to Romania, we had connected to an organization there—People to People—that helped to facilitate adoptions. Finally, the day arrived when we received permission from the US Immigration Service to bring children into our country.

Within a month, we were returning to Romania with such anticipation! Little did we know that our dream was disappearing before our very eyes. Our friend, Nicu, informed us that Romania had recently decided to ban all international adoptions. There had been problems for some years, and the whole "orphan adoption issue" was a political football. The door had been closed. Yet our heart to do something to help orphans in the world was still very much open.

Part One

Different Times, Different Places

A Young Boy's Life Interrupted
as told by Joseph
Chapter 1

Total Terror! "This was the worst lion attack that I could remember. I was too small to do anything about the attack except run for my life. I was able to get away by climbing up a tree where I stayed— too scared to say anything, or even to move. I knew I couldn't help my friend, but that made it even harder for me. I can actually remember seeing the lion eating my friend while I was up that tree! I was living a nightmare. Finally, after what seemed like several hours, the lion moved away from the tree I was in. I knew that even though I was still scared to death, I had to climb down and run for my life! I started to move like I was a grasshopper jumping quietly in the trees. I was afraid that if I made any noise, that lion would come back and attack me! I walked quietly at first, and then I ran as fast as I could to make it to a safe area where the rest of my friends were. In large numbers, where we were all together, the lion usually would not attack unless he was very hungry."

This was the scene in Southern Sudan, when

young Joseph's life was changed forever. He was about 10 years old, when he and his cousin, Paul (about 9) were outside the village tending the cattle with other boys their age. In a paper written for his first college English class he says, "I couldn't understand what was happening to me at that time. I could only see that people were fighting and shooting at us, resulting in many deaths. I could also see people running and hiding from the airplane that was shooting at us from above.

You see, we were under attack from our enemy, the Janjaweed (Southern Arabs), who were trying to get rid of the Christians. They were being supported in this effort by the government that was in power at the time. I could see some of my friends getting shot, while we were all trying to run away. That scared me very much and made me run faster than I ever had before--to get away from all the fighting. With each step toward the high grass, I felt some sense of safety ahead of me. I ran for my life just like I was taught to do when I heard the shooting. In those moments, I realized that I had learned something that would help me to get to the place where I would be safe. I learned that fear can take over your body, and you just react in the best way you know how. Fortunately for me, my family had taught us to run when we heard the fighting start, and that's all I could think about.

I can still picture myself sleeping on the grass while on my way to Ethiopia. I sometimes dreamed that I would wake up in the morning, heading safely on the road to my destination at the UN camp. I remember what we needed to do to survive on our trip. We had to climb up on fruit trees for our meals, when we were lucky enough to find a tree. We ate the fruit, whether it was ripe or not. We also had to fish in the river, although there were times when none of us could catch a fish—no matter how hungry we were. Insects were part of our diet, as well.

Hunger was not the only challenge we struggled with on our trek across Sudan. We experienced terrible tragedy while swimming crocodile infested rivers, including the Nile. At one point we witnessed one of our friends being eaten." (After he was comfortable with us, Joseph told us that he learned to swim—and fast—so a crocodile wouldn't have him for breakfast!).

"I often thought to myself (as I walked along the dusty, dry trail we followed) that if I gave up hope for getting to safety and for my future, I would never be able to help my people again. I was not interested then, nor am I interested now, in taking any revenge on those who killed my family and chased us out of my village. While I will not take revenge, I do want to get my education and one day go back to help my people. This would be an accomplishment that would be totally the opposite of what the Arabs would have wanted to happen from their efforts at genocide. Without successfully getting my education completed, I cannot accomplish my real goal. That is, to—one day—help my people rise up from the life they now have to become educated and successful. That would do more to neutralize what the Arabs were trying to do to us than anything else that I could do. One day, I will stand up and say to those who destroyed my family and my village, "Your efforts failed! We are not only still here, but we are even stronger than when you all tried to kill us." I believe that God will take care of the revenge aspect of the genocide, so that I don't have to."

After almost three months, the boys finally arrived at the Sherkole United Nations Refugee Camp in Ethiopia. Their hardship was still not over, though they would no longer have to fear for their lives. The camp was organized into different ethnic groups. When they came upon the other Mabaan refugees, they were made fun of and called "darsogia", which means desert people.

In order to receive food in the camp, they had to be given a ration card. It took them three months before they received theirs! When asked how they got food, they matter-of-factly said that some of their friends would share their meager amount of food with them. They were told to go to the home of the Dinka chief to receive their card. They showed up at the appointed time, only to be met by the chief who said he was sorry, but he had a problem and couldn't see them until the next day. The "problem" turned out to be a fight between his people and another tribe. By "fight", it meant attacking each other with knives and spears. Joseph and Paul ran and never returned!

One day, a worker from Save the Children/Sweden was riding his motorcycle through the camp. He came upon three Mabaan children digging in the dirt for yams. When he inquired about their activity, they told him that they needed food. He promptly secured a ration card for them. Then he found out that there were about 50 others that didn't have cards either, so he got them one. Joseph and Paul could now count on some food!

When Joseph and Paul showed up at the school in Sherkole, the teacher chased them away and told them that there wasn't room for them. That didn't set well with this dedicated worker from Save the Children/Sweden. He went with them to the school and got them enrolled. After Joseph was settled into his new American home, we looked on the internet to find Mabaan resources. We came across a website from a mission organization that was working in Sherkole. Joseph showed us his school—outside benches under a tree. His face beamed when he was able to see his teacher. They started learning English in the Sherkole Camp School, but the teacher had a strong British accent. This proved to be difficult for them.

"When I became comparatively comfortable in the UN Camp near Assossa, Ethiopia, I started to work outside in the surrounding area for a local bakery. I felt like my life was beginning all over again. My new surroundings were more comfortable than what I had while running for the last few months, but it was certainly not like home. At that point, I felt like an independent young man that had to make my own decisions, and that I needed to grow up fast. I learned that life is not easy, like a drink of water. I sometimes wondered why life was so difficult for me, but I didn't have much time to worry about the question. I still had dreams of being attacked again.

"My first food was grain and wheat. I was not used to having this kind of food, nor having to protect what I had to eat from theft. There were often fights in the UN camp for what little we had to eat. Some people even lost their lives in these fights. Even though it was not a perfect place, we, at least, had food and water and friends to share with there."

"After almost six years, my life was about to take another dramatic turn. I was asked by the Save the Children organization if I would be interested in being moved to Canada or America. Since I strongly desired educational opportunities, I agreed to undergo about 5 interviews with UNICEF workers. A friend came running up to me to tell me that he had seen my name on the chalkboard, as one of the people that would be able to go to America. He told me that the UN wanted to meet with me by the next day at 8:00 at their campus for an interview. I quickly confirmed that he was right and began my plans to leave my existing life behind. I think that because I told the American interviewer the truth about my life, I was one of the fortunate few (out of the 16,000 refugees in the camp) to be chosen to relocate to the USA."

"I was happy, then, to be selected to come to America, and I still am. However, even that had its challenges. The day before I left, I had to say goodbye to all of my friends. That was very difficult for me! That night I stayed up late talking to all of them. I can say, now, that my saying goodbye that night was the hardest moment of my life! To say goodbye, and know that I would not see my friends again was the most painful thing that I ever experienced. These friends were all I had in life, and soon they would no longer be there with me. Getting inside of that UN car, with tears coming down my cheeks is still difficult for me to think about. I tried to take a mental picture out of the car window, but we took off so fast, I could not do it. I did, none-the-less, see many of my friends with tears running down their cheeks. They turned around and left as the car sped away with me in it."

"I know my experiences and challenges from my youth have served to make me a better person than I would have been otherwise. I don't believe it is good to worry about what happened a long time ago. Instead, I want to work on making a better life for myself and for others, too."

From Calm to Chaos
Chapter 2

Adar, Sudan, 1990. Paul Yana faced the world—a much different world than we know. He was the youngest boy of a father with two wives. It is true that Christianity and long-standing cultural traditions sometimes clash. He had three older brothers— much older than he. By the other wife, Paul had two older stepsisters. His home was a mud hut. His mother and (sometimes) his father lived there with infant Paul. His father had another "home" for his other wife. Paul slept in his home until he was about four or five years old. At that time, his father built him a little hut where he would sleep with his friends. His older brothers already had homes of their own.

His life was happy then. He enjoyed playing in the sand with his friends and his cousin, Joseph, who was a year older. One of their favorite games was tag. They would chase each other and climb a tree as fast as they could—to get "free." Once, during this game, young Paul fell from the tree. When he got up, his arm was dangling crookedly! Not having a doctor in the village, a home remedy was in order.

They pulled his arm as straight as they could, and attached it to a straight piece of wood (their version of a splint). However, it was really swollen. To get the swelling down, they punctured holes in his arm and wrist with a sharp object which he described as something like broken glass. Blood came out, and the swelling went down. Unfortunately, he still has the scars where they punctured his arm. Also, his wrist doesn't rotate correctly because his arm healed without being set straight. Later, when he started school in the United States, he had the opportunity to learn to play the violin. However, with that arm permanently affected, he was unable to.

The peace and calm of his quiet life in Adar was disturbed by the death of his parents. They died from disease during his young life (about five years of age). His oldest brother and his wife became his caretakers. On his father's deathbed, he told young Paul that he wanted him to get an education. That was really important to his father. Therefore, at about six years of age, he and Joseph were sent to the government school for their education. Paul recalls that there was a lot of fighting between the different tribes attending. One time, a boy from another tribe took Paul's chair when he got up. A fight ensued. The teacher blamed Paul, so he got whipped!

The closest "government" school was about three hours away from their village, so the boys stayed in a dorm (at about six and seven years of age) during the week. Each weekend, they would walk the three hours back home. The difficult part was not the distance, rather that the government schools were Muslim schools. The teachers were constantly trying to persuade the boys to become Muslims. They offered to buy them new clothes and all the supplies they would need for school, if they would convert. Such pressure was particularly intense, given that school was closed on Friday and Saturday for the Muslim Sabbath. Joseph and Paul would walk to the village and spend the weekends with their families, which included worshiping on Sunday. They knew that every Monday morning, they would receive a whipping for missing school on Sunday. They sometimes wore more than one pair of pants, or something under their jeans to soften the blow. (They had to be careful, though, because if there was something too obvious, they would be whipped even harder). It was, apparently, common procedure to receive a crack of the whip. If they couldn't answer a question to the teacher's satisfaction, whack! Paul shared that one time he had an insect bite on his arm and was looking down at it and rubbing it. The teacher flogged him on that arm because he wasn't paying attention. That wasn't enough, but in front of the whole class, he said to Paul in a mocking tone of voice, "Does it hurt now, Paul?"

That fateful day when his village was attacked, Paul's life totally changed forever. At nine years old, he was on the run along with cousin Joseph and about 50 other boys. When the attack initially happened, he ran with his shoes on. However, they came off during the escape. The rest of the journey was done barefooted!

The scariest part of the "flight to freedom" for Paul was running at night. They also were careful to avoid roads and trails. The boys knew that if they ran in the daytime, they could be captured and forced to join the Arab army. The boys all fell many times because they couldn't see where they were going in the dark. The worst part was running into thorn bushes. When daylight arrived, they would help each other pull the thorns out of their skin!

Along with the fruit and fish they could find, they fed themselves from "gum" (Tem) trees. These were trees with a sticky sap-like substance. They would scrape the sap from the trees with a stick. This "gum" was sweet tasting and helped to sustain them. At times they would come across a farmer who was kindhearted enough to give the boys some food. Unfortunately, more often than not, the farmers and occasional villages that they came to would chase them away, like homeless people trying to crash a party.

Paul learned to be a good swimmer. As he said, "You had to be, so that the current wouldn't carry you away." Sometimes he got so tired from swimming that he would rest on a log and let it carry him along. When weariness would overtake him, he would have to give himself a pep talk. It went something like "I must make it or die!" Then he would realize that he wasn't in it alone. His friends were a great encouragement to him. To sum up his experience on the journey to safety, he said, "God was looking over me."

New Beginnings
Chapter 3

Divorce was not an option (though, at times, murder seemed like it)! That pretty much sums up our early marriage. It was June 19, 1976, in the Rose Garden at the First Baptist Church, Fresno, CA. I was a "bicentennial" bride. There were three very special guests (among the others) in attendance—Bruce's boys—Anthony (7 years old—almost 8), Craig (6) and my daughter, Kylee (4). This was a second marriage for us, and we were determined to make this one work!

Thus began our life, as baby Christians and as husband and wife. Little did we know the difficulties that lay ahead for us. We both have similar temperaments. Type A personalities and short fuses! I had been raised in a family where my mom had ruled the roost. Bruce, being a total Italian (both sets of grandparents had come over from Italy) just assumed that he was the ruler, or more fitting, the boss. Immediately, strong personality conflicts arose. We certainly hadn't yet learned that God's Word has great direction and guidance for marriage.

Then there was the stepparent thing. I didn't have a clue how difficult a job that would turn out to be. Neither Bruce nor I—though we had worked through the rejection of our divorces—realized how devastating divorce was for the children. Try as I did, I couldn't replace that deep longing for their biological mom. It didn't take us long to understand why God hates divorce. There are life-long consequences to endure when we don't do things His way.

Through all of the struggles, we wanted so much to raise our children as Christians. For three difficult years, we owned a business and tried to work together. In Bruce's background, his family had owned and operated restaurants for most of his life. Contrast that to my family—where my dad worked at the same job for 39 years, and we always knew exactly how much income to expect. How difficult it was for me to be the co-owner of the A&W restaurant in Oakhurst, CA! (I still refer to it as the A & "trouble you"). I'm not sure if I quit more times, or if he fired me more times. To say the least, it put a strain on our marriage. We did try to arrange our schedule so that if he opened early for breakfast, I'd come to work after the children were in school and work the later shift. He would then pick them up from school—or vise versa. We always took Sundays off, to go to church and have a family day.

After selling the restaurant, Bruce went into the insurance business. His career took off rapidly, and our family enjoyed the many benefits that he earned. We were blessed with some wonderful trips—sometimes for the two of us, and other times with the children included. I experienced my first cruise (to Mexico), trips to Disneyland, Vancouver, Sun Valley, St. Thomas, Hawaii, Hong Kong, and Munich. Traveling became a highlight of our life.

We were just completing our dream home in Bass Lake—on an acre plus that backed up to the Sierra National Forest. One day, as I was working on some of the finish staining, that dreaded phone call came. The company asked Bruce to become a regional manager in Southern California. I had been sensing some restlessness in Bruce, who loves a challenge. I froze on the spot! When I married him, I told him I'd go to the ends of the earth with him, but not Southern California! Needless to say, I learned never to say "never". After we talked, I cried out to the Lord, and it became clear that I wasn't to stand in the way of his career. Thus, we moved the family South when the kids were in 6th, 8th and 10th grades. This move added further strain on our marriage—as I'm ashamed to admit—my attitude was not what it should have been. I had a really difficult time leaving my beloved Sierra Nevada Mountains behind.

Our family finally adjusted to our new life, but the struggles of raising a blended family were still a challenge. Unfortunately, our marriage was still tumultuous, as well. After three years in the Southland, Bruce was asked to take a struggling region up in the Monterey Bay. By now, Anthony had graduated from high school, so our family of four moved to Watsonville. We could choose wherever we wanted to live within the Monterey Bay, so we chose a rural area outside of Watsonville. Meanwhile, our struggles continued. Finally, one day we looked at each other and agreed, "We say we're Christians, but our marriage doesn't look anything like a Christian marriage. We need help!"

We are forever grateful for Pastor Dave Harris who was the Associate Pastor of the church that we were attending at that time. He gladly gave of his time to help steer us on the right course. His homework for us was to pray together each day (a novel idea for us). It was amazing the change that this brought! My nagging, and our prayers just couldn't seem to co-exist. We were beginning to really communicate and turn from our selfish ways.

The Lord blessed our efforts and totally healed our marriage. It was an amazing transformation! Bruce was quickly becoming my best friend, rather than my adversary. Miraculously, the Lord began to use even us. He gave us a passion to help others not experience the pain and conflict that we had endured for so long. We started teaching marriage classes at our church and counseling couples who needed help. We were actually called upon to lead a few weekend marriage retreats for other churches. The Lord had replaced pain with a passion for marriage! Our big regret was that our children had grown up seeing our struggles. Though they have now left the nest, they have been able to see our love for each other and the healing that has taken place. We continually work hard to maintain our relationship.

Once our nest was emptied, we were really enjoying our time together! I finally stepped away from teaching and helped create our "Care Corps" ministry at church. We had a group of people with a heart, and we volunteered to help others with their issues—discipling them according to God's Word. It was thrilling to see many lives transformed before our very eyes!

Bruce and I still enjoyed traveling (and skiing) and got away every chance we could. Then we discovered short-term mission trips. What a joy it was to travel with a purpose! Our lives were changed forever, as we worked on many different projects. It's hard to explain the thrill involved in organizing and leading mission trips for fellow believers who had yet to experience serving in that way. The joy of being able to use our God-given talents and resources to benefit those less fortunate in the name of our Lord is an indescribable thrill! Little did we know that our greatest mission project would soon come to our home and change it for ever.

Part Two

Coming Together

Unaccompanied Refugee Minors
Chapter 1

After returning from our trip to Romania, we still felt that tugging on our hearts. The desire to care for some orphans was still very much alive. We had a subsequent meeting with BAAS, and they informed us that we weren't too old to seek out children from Russia. There was a new mound of paperwork to do. For some reason, that mound got pushed aside. Finally, one Sunday morning I said to Bruce, "We're not getting any younger, so if we're going to do this, we'd better sit down today and tackle this paper work." Then I added, "I don't really know why, but I have a hesitancy about this."

I went in to get dressed for church, when about five minutes later Bruce said, "Hey honey, come here. Check this out."

He was reading the San Jose Mercury News, and an ad jumped off the page to his attention. It was placed in the paper by the Catholic Charities of Santa Clara County. They were looking for foster parents for unaccompanied refugee minors. We both looked at each other and were totally on the same wave length. This would, indeed, be interesting to check out.

Bruce attended an informational meeting, but I had a prior commitment. He came home, having been impressed with the program, and especially the people in charge of it. Coleen Gulbraa from Catholic Charities did some of the presenting, as well as Terry Watters from Adopt International in San Francisco. These two organizations work together in this program. Adopt International actually acts as the legal guardians for the refugees, and Catholic Charities recruits and trains the foster parents. They also sponsor programs to assist the children and foster parents once they arrive.

After discussion and prayer, Bruce and I decided to sign on to the required training. We spent a few Friday nights and Saturdays up at the Catholic Charities headquarters in Santa Clara where we learned the ins and outs of fostering. The training contained a crash course in refugee children. During part of this training, we were introduced to two young men who were "lost boys of the Sudan." They shared with us about escaping from their village with many other boys, to get to safety in Ethiopia. After living there in a refugee camp for some time, war broke out in Ethiopia. They had to leave and take a long trek to Kenya. They shared about walking from one country to the next so matter-of-factly, as if it were a walk across town. They didn't display any bitterness or deep emotion, and in fact, had large smiles on their faces. They projected great warmth. We were awed, to say the least! The training was completed, along with another home study, and we were accepted as foster parents.

Then came the wait. Since there are many layers of bureaucracy involved, from the UN to the US Immigration Service to Adopt International and Catholic Charities, the process takes awhile. Not to worry. We were in the midst of finishing up our new home out in the country on the outskirts of Watsonville. It was on a twenty-acre farm that we had purchased a few years prior. We also continued to travel to Romania to work on more projects there. Bruce was seriously considering retirement from the insurance company that he had joined up with (which he did, in fact, at the beginning of the following year.) Life was good! Yet, there was still that anticipation and hope that we would be granted the privilege of doing something for a couple of orphans in the world.

Matthew 25

Chapter 2

The school year, 2005, was underway, and still no children were in the picture for us. There was hope that it wouldn't be long, since one of the other newly trained foster moms had welcomed three siblings from Sierra Leone into her home. Shortly thereafter, we received a call from Coleen at Catholic Charities saying that there were two young men from Southern Sudan—cousins—that had been accepted into the Unaccompanied Refugee Minor Program. Their names were Joseph Kelly and Paul Yana. They had been raised in a rural Christian village, and she thought that we would be a good match for them. We were provided with the sketchy information that was available. She even made a special trip down to our home along with Teresa Samuel-Boko, a young Sudanese lady (who would be our case manager). They came to answer our many questions. The reality of having foster children was setting in. I must admit that it was a bit scary. It would mean a total change in our lifestyle.

A short time elapsed, and then we were informed

that their arrival was imminent. We were to make our final decision and let them know by the following Monday.

All weekend long we agonized! We prayed, we talked, and we made mental lists of the pros and cons. Did we really want to tie ourselves down with youngsters in the house? Bruce's retirement was just months away, and we would be "foot loose and fancy free". We could continue to do short-term missions trips. Were we sure that this was really God's will for us? I was especially concerned about not being able to return to the Eastern European Bible College in Oradea, Romania, and continue teaching New Testament to the first-year students. This had become a yearly highlight for me. When Bruce suggested that we would just have to "tag-team" our mission efforts for a few years, I felt a bit better. So many questions and thoughts were swirling around in our minds that entire weekend!

Sunday morning arrived, and we were still in a state of confusion. We needed some clear direction, and we needed it soon! We went off to church, knowing that by the very next morning, our decision had to be made.

The singing was over, and we were seated. A young man from our congregation (one of my former students) got up to read the scripture for the morning. It was from Matthew 25. Verses 35 and 36 read, "For I was hungry and you gave me something to eat. I was thirsty and you gave me something to drink. *I was a stranger and you invited me in.* I needed clothes and you clothed me." . .

. (v. 40) The King will reply. "I tell you the truth, whatever you did to the least of these brothers of mine, you did for me." We looked at each other with tears in our eyes. God had spoken to us through His word! We left church that morning with a load taken from our shoulders. We were excited that in the near future our dream of helping a few orphans in the world would truly become reality.

Joseph
Chapter 3

The next week or two was a bustle of activity. The big bedroom that would be for the boys definitely needed some attention. Fancy white iron and brass daybeds would certainly not do well for the male gender. (Our two granddaughters were the thankful recipients of them). We found some nice wooden beds with pull-out mattresses underneath. (That way they could have friends over and our two grandsons would have a "bunk" when they came to visit). My best friend, Corine Kuykendall, went shopping with me for another dresser that would match the one we had. Coleen Gulbraa called us, in the midst of the preparations, to say that Joseph Kelly was arriving on Tuesday, September 27th, 2005, at the San Jose Airport. Our dream was becoming a reality—all too soon! The desks that had been ordered were—we were now told—not available for several weeks. No sweat. Bruce decided to make them by using two filing cabinets with a slab of left over granite from our son who is in the granite business. We had only one desk chair, so we would need another. While I was visiting a friend one day, she just happened to ask if I'd like the wooden chair she was getting rid of. God was beginning to provide in many specific ways.

We had been told in our training to have the rooms somewhat decorated when they arrived. This was due to the fact that everything would be so new to them, and they would be overwhelmed with such choices. Thanks to J.C. Penney, I found just the quilts and shams—with a mountain scene—ducks, bears, pine trees, etc.—that would nicely add a masculine touch. They were delivered just in time.

September 27 finally arrived! I still needed some window coverings, so I went shopping for the last touches. I wanted to make it look really inviting for the boys. On my way home, I stopped by to pick up a couple of balloons to take to the airport. One was red, white & blue with stars and stripes. The other said, "Welcome Home".

Bruce and I were really excited! As soon as the window valances were hung, we left for the airport. We stopped along the way to pick up our sweet daughter-in-law, Lili, who wanted to go along. She would certainly relate to the boys. She had just, over a year before, moved from Mexico City when she married our son.

We were met at the airport by Teresa Samuel-Boko, our Sudanese case-worker from Catholic Charities. There was such anticipation in the air! As the passengers disembarked from the plane, we nervously stared at each one. The wait seemed endless. Teresa told us that they would be easy to spot—"just look for two really skinny boys". Finally, after all the other passengers had filed past us, we spotted one young man. He had the darkest, most beautiful skin of anyone I had ever seen! He was thin, indeed, and carried with him only a plastic bag with some paper work in it. Teresa stepped forward and introduced herself and us to him. Though he looked a bit frightened, his big smile immediately captured us. Teresa then asked him, "Where is Paul?" He shrugged, and we realized that nobody knew. Somehow, Paul was lost in the bureaucratic shuffle. There stood Joseph—all alone, in a foreign land—being welcomed by complete strangers!

We headed for the car, and by now, it was dinnertime. Bruce had a great idea. We would stop at a buffet to eat—that way, Joseph could see the food and select what he wanted. (No menus to try to explain to someone with limited English). Our son, Tony, (Lili's husband) would meet us there. It just happened that our other son, Craig, who lived three hours South was in the vicinity picking up a load of granite. So he met us, too. Joseph got to meet his two new brothers right away.

Bruce walked Joseph through the abundant food lines, but he selected only plain white rice and plain spaghetti. His face lit up when he saw Tony come to the table with watermelon on his plate. Tony promptly went to get him some. Toward the end of our meal, Tony got up and brought back a dish of soft-serve ice cream for Joseph. He took one bite, and made a funny face. He wanted nothing to do with food that cold. Later, it dawned on us that there had been no refrigeration in his village in the

Sudan or in the refugee camp, either. He was not at all used to cold food.

Our next stop was to Target to buy some clothes. As we entered the store, Bruce decided to use the restroom. All of a sudden it dawned on him. Joseph had been on a long airplane flight. He had ridden 40 minutes to the restaurant. He had sat through a relaxed dinner, and we hadn't even thought to take him to a bathroom! (Just one of the "minor" things we missed in our training.) Needless to say, Joseph was "relieved" to be introduced to an American bathroom. We felt badly to have overlooked such an obvious detail.

After selecting necessary clothing—from underwear and socks to jeans, shirts, slippers, a jacket and a bathrobe—we were on our way home. It was bedtime by then, but there was one last detail that needed to be taken care of. After showing him around the house, a lesson on how to use the shower was in order. This was his first experience with such a "contraption." Sometime later, Bruce asked him how they bathed in Africa. He got to his knees by a "pretend" creek and pantomimed splashing himself with water. We all laughed.

The next morning, after a breakfast of oatmeal (we were told in training to feed them rather bland food at first until their stomachs were used to our rich foods), we headed back up to San Jose to meet Teresa. She took us, first, to the clinic where Joseph would receive 11 shots to begin his immunization process. As we waited for him to be called, ever the teacher, I started writing the ABC's. To my delight, he knew most of them, and we practiced words that started with the different letters. From there, we went to the Social Security Office where Teresa applied for his social security number. After stopping by for a Subway sandwich, we returned to the Catholic Charities office. We would be met there by Terry Watters from Adopt International. By law, he had to read him his rights according to the foster care rules. To this day, we don't know how much he really understood.

Finally, after what must have been an exhausting day for him, we headed back down the hill toward Watsonville. Having already arrived when we got home, my sister, Kitty, (really Margaret) was here for a visit. She had moved to Montana that summer and was back for her good-byes. Joseph was able to meet his new Aunt. Both of us had been raised in an era and a place where racial prejudice was all too often the norm. Before she left, we chatted about the changes in America in our lifetime. We both questioned whether even our own mother would have accepted an African boy into the family. Also on hand to greet him were our two little kittens, Tabby and Butterscotch.

From Joseph's View

Joseph was told to report by 6:00 the next morning. Paul accompanied him to the bus to say goodbye and wish him well. Fortunately for Joseph, three of his friends were also chosen. He wouldn't have to board the bus alone. Though Paul was sad to see him go, he was happy that Joseph had the opportunity. Besides, Paul had a lot of friends in the camp, which made it less difficult for him.

They were taken by bus to Assosa and then flown to Addis Ababa. In Addis Ababa, UNICEF and IOM (International Organization for Migration) provided money for them to eat. They stayed at night in private homes, and hung around the market during the day. Finally, after about a week, the IOM gave them a bag with their papers in it. Off they were taken to the Addis Ababa Airport. It was late at night when the airplane lifted off toward London.

Upon arrival in London, they were sent off of the airplane and had to wait for three hours to board their next flight. This was the good-bye place for two of the boys who were being sent on different airplanes—one to Philadelphia and one to Laughlin, Nevada. Finally, Joseph and his friend, Santino, departed from London and flew across the ocean to New York City. They were met there by a UNICEF worker and taken to a hotel to spend the night. They had to get up early the next morning and got a little confused as to where to catch the shuttle. They went up the stairs instead of down. Finally, they figured out where to go. At the airport Joseph had to say good-bye to Santino because he was headed for Texas. From New York, he flew all by himself to Chicago. Joseph was totally alone in a strange country.

When he landed in Chicago, he didn't know quite where to go. He showed his ticket to a friendly looking person who pointed him in the right direction. When he arrived at the gate, he handed his ticket to the lady. She promptly gave it back to him and explained that he would have to wait about 30 minutes for his flight. A kind gentleman beckoned him over to sit with him until it was time. When the man got up with his ticket, Joseph followed. He handed his ticket to the lady, and watched "the machine eat it up—all but a little piece."

He was finally on his way to San Jose. He didn't eat on the airplane because he was feeling sick to his stomach. He sat on the plane until most of the passengers had disembarked. Finally, he took the courageous walk to meet his new family. He remembers seeing us (and the balloons), and thinking that we were going to be his new parents.

One time when we were talking about his experiences, and complimenting him on his great courage, I asked, "How did you get picked to come to America over all of the kids in the camp that had to be left behind?"

He answered, "God picked me!"

Settling In

Chapter 4

The next day, we had time to stay around town. I asked my sister what she'd like to do, and she chose a drive down the coast to Castroville. We always enjoyed the deep fried artichoke hearts at the "Giant Artichoke". It was Joseph's first glimpse of the Pacific Ocean, and he was taking it all in as we drove. When we were seated and handed menus, I realized that I'd have to help Joseph. Of course, he didn't know how to read it, much less, what all the different choices were. I thought, "What would a teenage boy really enjoy?" Of course, a cheeseburger! It turned out to be a great choice, as evidenced by the smile on his face as he rapidly devoured it. (It was the beginning of his love affair with burgers.) The French fried artichoke hearts didn't appeal as much. One idea that we had early on was that when I served a meal, we asked Joseph to rate how well he liked it on a scale of 1-10. (1 was he didn't like it, up to 10—it was great.) That was really a help for me to know better what to cook for him. The stuffed bell peppers that I made one evening were the only 1 I can remember, whereas pizza has been a 10 from the start.

Teresa came down the following day to get him signed up for his medical benefits, which are part of the program. It was Joseph's second time of waiting for your name to be called. We used the time to work on English words, naming such items as watch, earring, etc. We shopped a bit more for some of the items he still needed, before heading home. That afternoon began the process of "tagging our house". We made an ABC book for Joseph, and he wrote the words in it. I wrote them on a sticky to attach to the object—chair, table, bedroom, stove, etc. Each day for the next few weeks, we would add stickies and have little quizzes on the different rooms and items in our home. I introduced him to the microwave by putting some water out of the tap into a cup and having him touch it. I then placed it in the microwave for about 30 seconds and had him touch it again. There was definitely a surprised look on his face. He learned about the mixer and the oven by helping me to make a batch of cookies.

On Friday morning, we had to go to the Doctor's office to have the TB test read. Thankfully, our family physician agreed to look at it, which saved hours of driving to the clinic up in San Jose. What a phenomenon Joseph created! As he was escorted into one of the rooms, four of the office personnel all came in to meet him. They had many questions—most of which he didn't understand—so I gave them a short summary of his background. They all gave him a royal welcome and were genuinely interested in this special young man. One of the most common questions asked was, "How old is he?" The answer (we thought) was 16, but he didn't come with any knowledge of his birthday or any record of his birth. The government gives each of the refugees the birthday of 1/1 of whatever year they were thought to have been born. (In his case, 1989). Due to the lack of educational opportunities, he was in about 5th grade in the Mabaan language and culture. This artificial birthdate of January 1st would be a disadvantage, because it probably made him older than he really was.

That afternoon, we had been invited to a surprise "happy teen-age birthday/swimming party" for Taylor Noonan, a sweet young lady at our church that we had known since she was a baby. Both my sister and Joseph went along with us. Joseph was greeted warmly. Though the teenage boys came up to meet him and say hello, it seemed a bit awkward for them due to the language barrier. He wasn't really included in much of the pool play. He sure enjoyed the grilled cheeseburgers, though!

My sister left early the next morning. She had grown fond of Joseph in these few days. After my return from the airport, Joseph and I headed to the annual "Walk for Life" sponsored by the Pregnancy Resource Center. I thought he would enjoy this, and I was anxious to introduce him to my friends who were there. (I had recently served a two-year stint on the Board and had worked with many wonderful people). The Walk was held in Santa Cruz, along West Cliff Drive with awesome views of the ocean below. He seemed to thoroughly enjoy the rolling waves, rocks, and the refreshing ocean air. They had lots of food for the walkers, and he got to meet some really nice young men his age. It turned out to be a wonderful experience for us.

It was now Joseph's first Sunday in America. We had our breakfast and headed off to church. He received a really warm welcome, and Pastor Dennis Smith introduced him from the pulpit. Many shook his hand after the service. We noticed him showing some people the place on the big map at the back of the foyer where his village in Sudan was located. He immediately made friends with a wonderful couple from Africa. We invited them for dinner shortly after Joseph's arrival. They showed up with a really nice pair of dress pants and shirt for him.

One morning during his first few days with us, our contractor, Keith Pharris (who was still finishing up some work on our new home) came in for a cup of coffee. He was so friendly to Joseph and was genuinely interested in him. That afternoon, after he returned from his lunch break, he brought a couple of bags of really nice clothing items that his stepson no longer could wear. There were shirts, shorts, pants, a jacket, etc. That large grin of Joseph's was even bigger when he realized they were all for him! A short time after his arrival, we received a really nice card with a check enclosed from my dear college friend and sorority sister, Carol Richie and her husband, Doug. We were beginning to witness the many blessings that would lie ahead for us!

I was totally unprepared for the "celebrity" status with which he was received. People in the grocery store would stop and ask him where he was from and welcome him to the United States. He always maintained that ear to ear smile! The most humorous incident happened one day as we stopped in at Taco Bell. A man—total stranger—walked up next to us in line and said, "Hey, is that the kid from Sudan?" He realized from the puzzled look on my face that I was surprised a total stranger knew about Joseph. He added, "My girlfriend's daughter works at your doctor's office, and she told me all about him." With that, he reached his hand out with a huge, friendly smile, and said to Joseph, "Welcome!"

While on the subject of Taco Bell, a solemn moment occurred a few weeks later. Bruce and Joseph were working on a project out in the workshop and needed some supplies. After running their errands, they drove into the drive-thru. About that time, a small airplane flew overhead on its way back to the Watsonville Airport. Joseph looked up, cowered somewhat, and said in clear English, "airplane".

"Yes," Bruce replied, "our airport is just over there."

Joseph answered, "Airplanes come to our village with a black box on the side and go bang! bang! bang!" Needless to say, Bruce held back a tear.

A more humorous event occurred one day as I was in the kitchen. Joseph came in and told me that he needed some "poop" for the bathroom. I held back a snicker and tried hard to understand what he meant. Somewhat exasperated that I didn't know what he meant, he went into the bathroom and came back holding an empty "shampoo" bottle!

Meanwhile, we still had no word about Paul. Each day we would pray, "Lord, please bring Paul to us."

School

Chapter 5

It was now Joseph's first Monday in America. His immunizations and social services were all secured, and it was time to enroll him in school. After careful consideration and prayer, we decided that the Pacific Coast Charter School would be the best for him. It offered independent study under the guidance of a teacher. A couple of teenage girls at the church had attended there and spoke highly of the school.

As the door of the elevator opened, both of us were a bit nervous. We approached the principal's office and were greeted with several warm smiles. The lady in the front office was someone I had known, but had not seen for several years. She gave me the necessary application forms. A few friendly teachers came to meet Joseph. I answered questions that Vicki Carr, the principal, asked. It was decided that I should return the next day with all of the forms filled out.

At the appointed time, we returned and were re-introduced to one of the friendly faces we had met the day before—Debra Leigh. She was to be

Joseph's teacher for the school year. She and the principal helped me select textbooks—Phonics, Reading, Language Development and Math, along with maps, globes, and manipulatives. I came home loaded with wonderful materials to begin helping Joseph learn more English. We would meet each week with Debra to monitor progress and procure more material as needed.

In addition, there were some classes held at the school—one of which was ceramics. Joseph's eyes lit up when we went into the art lab and spotted the potter's wheel. He would come each Friday morning for class. Soon, my shelves at home were decorated with his artistic creations. Also, one of the students who enjoyed track and field events—with his mother's supervision—had a running and physical activity class after school twice a week. They met at a local middle school field. Joseph was neck-in-neck with William as they ran their laps around the field. He really looked forward to Tuesday and Friday afternoons!

Debra Leigh was such an outstanding teacher! It was obvious from the get-go that she was really fond of Joseph. One weekend, shortly after Joseph became her student, she and her husband took a trip to Yosemite. While there, she bought him a beautiful 60-piece concentration game with photos of Yosemite. He really enjoyed matching up the two "like" photos and could remember where they were. To this day, I've never defeated him at that game. Debra has a love of birds, and she gave Joseph her bird-caller gadget. He would place a picture of a certain bird in it, and the bird's call would play out loud. He would laugh! She also helped him with computer skills. The school provided him with a wonderful program to learn the keyboard, as well as a link to Rosetta Stone—a program that helped him with English.

Our work at home began each morning with reading from a beautifully illustrated children's Bible that Debra gave him. (She found it out in her garage when she was cleaning). We spent a lot of time on phonics, so that Joseph would learn the English sounds. We started at about 8:30 am. and worked through the morning. He would take breaks and ride my bicycle around the place, or run down to the barn. After lunch, we would continue with Math and Social Studies. I wanted him to learn a bit about American history. He was such a willing student. We were both wishing that Paul were here to get started on the curriculum, too.

Being a home school mom was a big adjustment for me, though I was enjoying the challenge. I had been involved in the "Care Corps" ministry at our church, as well as women's Bible study. I took an aerobics class three times a week, Romanian language lessons, and had time to go to lunch with my friends, talk on the phone, etc. I also enjoyed being a substitute teacher at the nearby Monte Vista Christian School. All of this had to be put on hold for a while. At times, I really felt out of touch, but this wouldn't be permanent.

More Settling In
Chapter 6

About a week before Joseph arrived, our friend, Mary Silveria, had gone to a garage sale. She found a guitar that was like new, and couldn't resist buying it. One Sunday, she approached us in church and asked if we would like to have it for the boys. We jumped at the chance, paid her back for her investment, and had a guitar here waiting when Joseph arrived.

Another close friend, Cal Hicks—a fabulous guitar player who blesses us each Sunday with his wonderful playing in church—has a ministry of offering free lessons to young men. He has worked with several boys who needed a mentor and were reached for the Kingdom because he offered his time to teach them the guitar. He took Joseph as one of his students. Each week, we would drive him to Cal's home for a lesson. He seemed to really enjoy it.

The second week after his arrival, Bruce and I were going to be in a wedding of our friends, Harold and Cindy Brockman. The evening of the rehearsal dinner, it so happened that Donnie Moore and his team from Radical Reality were going to be out at the county fairgrounds for a rally. Our youth leaders— Scott and Kellie Hubbard—agreed to have us leave Joseph off at their home, and they would take him out to the fairgrounds with them. Their son, Ian, is about the same age. We would meet out there after the rehearsal dinner. Joseph's eyes surely "got big" as Donnie and his team broke bricks and ripped phone books in half! He was thrilled to receive a signed picture poster of the entire Radical Reality team. It still hangs on their bedroom wall today.

The next evening was the wedding. Of course, we had to go that afternoon to get dressed with the bridal party. We took Joseph along and put him in charge of the camera. He was fascinated at the "tiny, little box" that could capture special moments. He took pictures of the ceremony, and really seemed to enjoy that responsibility. The reception was a lovely buffet dinner, which he also seemed to like. There was more food on each plate than Joseph was used to seeing in a month! After the meal, the music began. I asked Joseph if he wanted to dance with me. He seemed to get all embarrassed and wouldn't budge from his seat (even with my pleading). Suddenly, a lady that we didn't even know, from the next table over, got up, grabbed Joseph by both arms and dragged him out onto the dance floor. She wasn't going to take no for an answer! I knew he was okay with it when I saw that big grin appear on his face. As I watched him at his first American dance, it was obvious that music and dancing were part of who this young man was. I couldn't help myself. I cut in and had a great dance partner for the rest of the evening.

We hadn't found anyone who speaks Mabaan, so Joseph was totally immersed in English. He had mentioned to us that he had brought a Mabaan Bible to the US with him. However, he had given it to Santino in New York, before he took a flight to Texas to start his new life. We were able to find some web sights that had entries for "Mabaan" with the help of Debra and a friend of Joseph's at school. On one of these sites, we came across Aurora Ministries out of Bradenton, Florida. They produce audio-tapes for blind people and have the Bible translated into many languages. One of them was Mabaan. Bruce e-mailed them and explained Joseph's situation. Though they normally only send the tapes to blind people, when they read about Joseph's plight, they graciously agreed to send him a Mabaan Bible on cassette tape. What excitement was in the air, the day the tapes arrived and he opened the box! During his free time that afternoon, I heard the sound of a "strange" language coming from his room. The sounds were accompanied by that huge grin on his face.

One of our dearest friends, Dale Kuykendall, drives a big rig for the farmer he works for. Often, he moves tractors and other equipment to various locations. One day he called while Joseph and I were working away at our school. Would Joseph like to ride in the big truck with him? I drove him to meet Dale and noticed an especially large grin as he climbed into the cab of the big rig. He really enjoyed himself, and it didn't hurt that they stopped for a cheeseburger at lunchtime. Afterward, we asked him if he thought he might like to drive a truck someday. He answered in the negative. That truck was just too big for him. He had hardly experienced automobiles, much less a truck that huge. It was beyond his comprehension to drive something so large.

Wanting to teach Joseph about some of the American traditions, we found ourselves in a pumpkin patch one afternoon. He helped me pick a couple of nice ones. Upon our return home, we began his first lesson in jack-o-lantern carving. Bruce came out to help him, and before long we had a couple of good looking (not at all scary) pumpkin faces to display on our front porch. Joseph's artistic talent was surfacing once again. Butterscotch and Tabby, our kittens, got right in there to help. He seemed quite proud of his finished product.

On Saturdays we usually worked around the place. It was plain to see that Joseph really enjoyed working alongside of Bruce with all the tools in his shop. In fact, one afternoon when I had returned home, I found Joseph in my laundry room assembling a cabinet—all by himself! He had helped Bruce work on putting together some items for the new home, and had learned really rapidly.

When we had moved into our home about four months before, we had our baby grand player piano moved out into our extra garage. The plan was to strip it and re-stain it to a lighter finish. It required a lot of "elbow grease" sanding it down to remove the dark finish. Joseph was working alongside me for quite a long time. It certainly wasn't a particularly fun job. That evening at dinner, I apologized to him that we had had to work so hard most of the day. He looked at me with a rather funny expression and said, "That wasn't hard work". He then explained that while he was in the refugee camp, in addition to the bakery job, he had also worked for a farmer weeding the sorghum fields from 6 a.m. until 6 p.m. every Saturday. Most times the farmer wouldn't allow a break, and blisters were not an acceptable excuse to slow them down. One time, Joseph, Paul, and a group of their friends labored all day for a farmer. After all their work, he chased them off without paying them. With the money he earned, (when he got paid) he could purchase clothes and additional food. He shared that it would take him a couple of week's wages to be able to buy a pair of jeans.

One weekend that fall, we drove down to Nipomo (about three hours south of us) to visit our grandchildren and watch them play soccer. It was Joseph's first opportunity to meet Bruce's parents, sisters, and his new nieces and nephews—Andrew (14), Amber (11), Dominic (6) and Kaitlin (4). It was obvious right away that he has a great love for children. He truly enjoyed their games, and especially playing soccer with them afterward. He also learned how to play pool that weekend. Grandma and Grandpa Bruscia had a pool table, which he thoroughly enjoyed. He had a great time playing with their little "mutt", Butch, too.

Though Joseph was adjusting to his new American life, we could tell that it was pretty lonely for him at times. We continued to pray for Paul's arrival.

Paul, at Last!
Chapter 7

Toward the end of October, the long anticipated call finally came. Paul Yana would arrive at the San Jose Airport on Friday, Nov. 4, 2005. Our prayer was answered (and Joseph was quite excited). We sure looked forward to the arrival of our second son.

When we got to the airport, we were met not only by Teresa, but also by Sister Marilyn Lacey, who was in charge of the entire Refugee Resettlement program for Catholic Charities. As with Joseph's arrival, we had balloons to welcome Paul to America, too. Again, we waited with anxious expectation for the passengers to file past us. We were somewhat concerned when the pilot and stewardesses walked by. We asked if there was a young black boy on the plane. We were told that he was the last one off. Finally, we spotted him! He was smaller than Joseph, and I was struck by his gaunt appearance. He weighed in at 105 lbs. at 15 years old. What we weren't aware of was the fact that Paul had no idea that he was coming to be with Joseph. What an emotional moment when he spotted his cousin. His mouth dropped open and he exclaimed, "JOSEPH!!!" There wasn't a dry eye for us onlookers.

Paul also hadn't eaten on the plane, and it was past lunchtime. We bought him his first American burger in the airport, but his stomach was in too much turmoil to enjoy it. Teresa whisked us off to the clinic, since it was Friday, and immunizations needed to commence immediately. I felt so badly for Paul. It was like, Welcome to America, now get poked in the arm seven times! When we left the clinic, we headed down toward Gilroy to do some clothes shopping. Paul and Joseph chattered in Mabaan the entire time. Sadly, as we pulled up to the parking lot of Wal-Mart, Paul got sick. Apparently, the burger and the shots hadn't been such a good mixture. After freshening up in the bathroom, we helped him pick out some of the necessary clothing items.

It was dinnertime when we finished, and three of us were hungry. Paul really didn't want anything, but we ordered him some oatmeal, thinking that would help settle his stomach. He looked so tired and somewhat miserable, and just couldn't eat too much.

When we arrived home, Joseph gave him the tour and helped him settle in. He was excited to show Paul the modern inventions that he had never experienced--like a warm, American shower. So many of the things we take for granted were fresh, exciting new novelties to these young men.

The next day, poor Paul hardly ate anything, and I was getting somewhat concerned. He seemed in a daze and was suffering from jet lag. He was able to rest quite a bit. Joseph had him outside trying to ride Bruce's bicycle. After a little practice, it all came back to him. We later learned that there were a few bicycles in Sherkole, but they had to pay money to ride them. Paul, too, was introduced to Bruce's tool shop. Since this was a Saturday, here was the beginning of a whole bunch of male bonding going on out in that shop!

One memorable moment that weekend was when Paul saw me load dirty dishes into the dishwasher. When I put the soap in and turned it on, he just stood there laughing as he realized that the "white box with the door" would wash all those dishes!

On Sunday morning, thankfully, he ate his bowl of oatmeal and asked for more. From that time on, his appetite kicked in. He was also welcomed from the pulpit in church that Sunday, and he received a huge applause. Pastor Dennis explained that Paul thought he would never see Joseph again, but how God had reunited them at the airport.

The following morning, I took Paul along with Joseph to get him enrolled in school. Everyone had been waiting anxiously to meet "Joseph's cousin." Debra Leigh was Paul's teacher, too; and loaded us up with more books and resources. Paul didn't want to take the ceramics class, so he and I would hang out, usually at the grocery store, after we left Joseph off. At other times, he would choose to stay in the computer lab while Joseph was in ceramics class. He liked the track and running class a lot, too. Debra also worked with both boys on Wednesday mornings, and arranged for another of her students—Kelly McGuckin—to help them. She became a really good friend to the boys. At the end of the school year, all three of them received special awards of achievement at the graduation ceremony.

Meanwhile at home, work progressed. I had a contest between the boys to see which one could first say in English an object around the house that I pointed to. They were progressing well through the phonics and language workbooks, as well as the readers. They actually advanced three levels in reading by the time the school year was up.

Three mornings a week, Bruce would wake them up at 6:00, and the three of them would go to the Spa Fitness Center to play racquetball and work out. They would come home between 8:00 and 8:30 for breakfast, and then we would start our school. Paul seemed to really enjoy the stories from that beautifully illustrated children's Bible that Debra had given them. Whenever we came across an unfamiliar English word, we would enter it in their ABC vocabulary books along with the meaning. We would work on reading and language until about 10:30, at which time they would go outside for a break. Math came after that until lunchtime. In the afternoons, we would work on American history and some Science. They were eager students. The homeschool teacher was still adjusting to little time for herself and missing some of the activities that she was used to. The many home school moms from our church were really encouraging to me, which helped quite a bit.

One day, during Paul's first week, we took a day of celebration and went to visit the Monterey Bay Aquarium. The boys had such big smiles as they touched starfish and watched the colorful jellyfish. My friend, Corine, was taking care of her two grandchildren from Texas, so they went with us. Paul—like Joseph really relates well to children, and they all had fun together. On the way home, we stopped for a chocolate-dipped ice cream bar at Costco. Paul took one bite and made a face like Joseph did when he first tasted cold food. He wouldn't eat the rest. Like Joseph, he has since gotten over his distaste for ice cream.

Paul also started to take guitar lessons, and he enjoyed them a lot. One day, Cal asked if he could hire the boys to move a rather large pile of wood from one place on his property to another. As they labored, Cal and his wife, Julia, were amazed at the neat way it was all stacked up. They were pleased with how hard the boys had worked with little supervision.

They were also earning money, as Bruce hired them to do odd jobs around the farm—for $10.00 per hour. Saturdays found them painting, weeding, etc. They were learning how to use tools and fix things. Before their first year was up, both boys could actually weld (and as Bruce would add—a cleaner weld than he could do). They both had bank accounts and were saving a lot of their money. They enjoyed spending some of it, too. Paul is a bit more frugal, but they both like buying clothes. Speaking of clothes, our friends, Walt and Robin Combs, had gone out shopping for the boys and brought over jeans and shirts for both of them. We received a package from Idaho one day, for the boys. My sorority sister from college and her husband—Chris and Mary Howard—sent really nice knit snow hats for them. They knew it wouldn't be long before we took them to the snow. The many blessings were continuing!

A new family at our church—the Gullmams-- soon became good friends. After raising their own six children (the youngest of which was a junior in high school), the parents adopted four siblings from the Foster Care system. We had all seven of them over for dinner shortly after Paul's arrival. The four youngest Gullmans really took to Joseph and Paul. Most Sunday mornings, our boys were seated between their four. Since the Gullman's enjoy tie-dying, they made Joseph and Paul tie-dyed shirts.

Little did we know that our union with the boys would shed a new light for us on the entire subject of discrimination. While we've seen very little negative discrimination, we have experienced it in a subtle form, which is more a recognition of our differences. A common example is when we would walk into a store with the boys, more often than not, the clerk would ask us if we need help. When we said that we were just looking around, they would then ask the boys if they needed help. It didn't dawn on them that we were all together. We have even heard people asking them what their African names were. Thankfully, our overall experience has been overwhelmingly positive.

Paul was settling into the family very nicely. Though he is more serious by nature than Joseph, he possesses a great sense of humor. When something tickles him, he laughs with his entire being, and everyone else breaks out into laughter, too! Both Bruce and I were enjoying the sounds of young folks laughing in our home. It made things come so alive! We found that both boys have such sweet, sensitive spirits.

From Paul's View

After Paul had seen Joseph get on the bus, he settled back into his life at Sherkole UN Camp. He wondered how Joseph was doing and if he would ever see him again. Thankfully, after a few weeks, his name appeared on the list to come to the United States. He stayed about two more weeks and was able to say his good-byes to all of his friends there. Then the day arrived when the bus came for him. Unlike Joseph, he didn't have friends leaving with him. The others—a Dinka lady and her four children (ages about 6 to 16) along with a Dinka young man of about 18 boarded the bus. Fortunately, they could communicate in Arabic. Unfortunately, the other young man smoked and drank, so Paul didn't have much in common with him.

After they arrived in Addis Ababa, they had to wait for two weeks while their paper work was being done. They were able to stay in a hotel and got their meals provided. To Paul, the two weeks wait was really boring. Finally, they were told that they should be ready to be transported to the airport around 6 o'clock in the evening. However, they had to wait 2 or 3 more hours for the IOM to come. Finally, they arrived at the airport, and Paul was on his way to London. From London, he had to fly—all by himself to Chicago. A lady from the IOM met him in Chicago where he stayed—all alone—in a hotel. The hotel had a shuttle that took him to the airport, and again, he was assisted by an IOM worker.

The last leg of his journey to San Jose began. He remembers being very sleepy and only had some tea on the flight. The lady next to him handed him some grapes and insisted that he eat them. When the plane descended into San Jose, Paul got off and started following the crowd. However, he saw some people in the airport sitting and others going in different directions. He promptly turned around and headed back to the plane. A man asked him if he needed help, so Paul followed him. Suddenly he saw Joseph and thought to himself, "What is he doing here?" It took him a short time to realize that they were actually going to be together. When I asked him about seeing us for the first time, he said that he didn't really notice us. Once he laid eyes on Joseph, that's all that mattered to him!

Every so often he gets a call from the Dinka woman with the four children. They settled first in South Dakota, but since have relocated to Nebraska. They seem to be enjoying their life in the United States.

First Thanksgiving
Chapter 8

The first American holiday for the boys was approaching rapidly. We were reading about the Pilgrims and the Mayflower in our history book. Also, my collection of Pilgrim statues, cornucopias, and "autumn décor" was adorning our home.

Since this was the "off" year for our son Craig and his family (our four grandchildren), I decided to invite our African friends and their young sons. He shared with us that he had actually been helped through Catholic Charities of Santa Clara County when he first came to America. We also had our son, Tony, over. (Lili was visiting her family in Mexico City).

The looks of delight on Joseph and Paul's faces when they took their first bites of the turkey were priceless. Turkey turned out to be one of their favorite meals, and they ask for it ever so often.

Our tradition of going around the table and sharing what we are thankful for was introduced to the boys. My heart was touched when Paul said he was thankful for his new "mom and dad". It was the first time that he used this title, because they ordinarily call us Bruce and Sue.

After dinner, all the boys (which included Bruce) played soccer to work off some of their dinner before the pumpkin and pecan pies. It was a really pleasant day. We were truly touched, when our son, Tony, went home and wrote the following letter to the editor of the Hollister newspaper:

What Does it Mean to be Thankful?

I had a remarkable experience this Thanksgiving. It started out normal, heading to my parent's house, anticipating all the great food my mom makes every year. But this year was very different, and it left me full of more than just good food.

My parents recently became foster parents to two boys from Sudan, Africa, ages 15 and 16. Joseph and Paul are so naïve to our American ways that they are like babies. And yet, they are more like men than most Americans will ever be. I can't begin to understand the experiences they have had, for my life has been far too easy, and I have been so blessed. This was their first Thanksgiving, or any other holiday here.

My parents also invited friends from their church, who are originally from Congo, Africa. Their names are African (Ikin and Ulsya Hopa), but you can see how they have become African Americans. They are pursuing the "American dream" with two young boys, owning a home, and discussing real estate investing with my father and I. The Hopas must be a comfort and an inspiration to Joseph and Paul who feel a little like "fish out of water."

Like most Americans, we have our traditions. We like to go for a walk to "work off our dinner" (who are we kidding?), and most importantly, we take turns sharing what we are thankful for. This year, we played soccer (futbol) instead of walking (surely burning more calories) and like always we shared what we are thankful for. I am usually not short of words, but I found myself almost overwhelmed, and I didn't know quite what to say. The thoughts were swirling in my head as we had just finished stuffing ourselves with more food than some people might see in a month. But most importantly, instead of being anonymous and in a far off land, those "some people" were sitting at our table. Those "some people" were my brothers and friends. I've never had to worry about having food to eat, and I've never had my family all murdered by rebels. I've never spent more than a month walking across my country to get to another country where I could spend 6 years in a refugee camp, dreaming of the opportunity to live in America. Can you even imagine? Stop for a moment and try . . .

My father's sentiments were right on, but he too spoke clumsily. He only wishes he knew how to be thankful like them. Ikin was quick to correct my father and said, "No, you don't want to have the experiences we have had." But the burning question in my mind is how can we be thankful when we don't know what it's like? It's easy to believe that true happiness comes from success (which is a euphemism for having material things), but are we slaves to our materialism? I have always enjoyed nice cars and houses, and all the material things of this world. But how much is enough? I don't know. I have some friends who are well off, and I know they struggle to teach their children to not take things for granted. Will their children be able to be thankful, and how can they ever have the gratefulness that comes from having so little? I do know that I should be so much more thankful than I am, and I am thankful for Joseph, Paul, and the Hopas. And so much more . . .

Tony Bruscia

Hollister

The next morning, we got up very early to leave

for a short jaunt to Yosemite. Both boys enjoyed playing the Concentration game so much, and the gorgeous scenes of Yosemite on the game cards were spectacular! We had promised to take them there as soon as time permitted, and that was now.

We arrived at the Big Trees in time to meet our long-time friends, Glenn and Carol Finks who live in Coarsegold. Glenn is actually a tour guide in Yosemite, so he gave us (and their relatives who were with them) his interesting and informative talk. I so enjoyed watching the boys look up at the awesome trees.

We drove down toward Yosemite valley, but it was really crowded. There was a lot of road work going on, and traffic was moving at a snail's pace. It also had started raining. After a short while, we decided to drive down to the Highway 140 exit and find our hotel located outside of the Park. We spent a relaxing evening playing UNO and watching a movie on TV.

Speaking of movies, we have had so much fun with the boys and movies. At first, when the boys saw a movie, we didn't realize that they thought they were watching a recording of something that really happened. Imagination was not something they could relate to. When they witnessed a fight or action scene, they thought it was real. We first realized this when they saw the same actor the second time. They said, "Wait! He died in the last movie we saw!" Bruce explained that what they were seeing wasn't really happening, that movies are make believe, and it takes the viewers imagination to make them work. It took them a lot of questions and a really long time to understand. Often the boys talk to the characters in the movies, as if they could hear them. When something is funny in a movie, they laugh with so much abandon, that we end up laughing more at them than the movie.

The next morning, we drove to Hetch Hetchy (a place that Bruce and I had never seen). On the way, Paul spotted a few deer. We thoroughly enjoyed hiking around there and soaking up the beautiful sunshine. As we were ascending the mountain back toward the valley, to our delight, we saw a bear at the side of the road. (It's not usual to have a bear sighting). I just thanked the Lord for showing His great love for us in yet another way!

This day was much nicer than the day before, so we were able to take in the attractions of the Valley—Yosemite Falls, the Village and movie at the visitor center, as well as the Ahwahnee Hotel. On our way back home, we promised a return trip in the spring when there would be lots more water in the falls, and we would include our bicycles.

Snow

Chapter 9

We were now well into the holiday season. The boys had helped us pick out our Christmas tree and decorate it. The whole house took on a festive look for the holidays. Some friends who have access to a time-share condo in Lake Tahoe had asked us to join them one weekend before Christmas. This would be the boys' first exposure to snow. We wanted to give them the opportunity to learn to ski since we enjoy it so much. Mills and Sephie Miracle brought Mills' daughter, Michelle, and Sephie's daughter, Mayra, along. Mayra was a friend to the boys because she was in the youth group at our church. Michelle, who is African American and had been adopted by Mills, was a super young woman. We all had fun with her, though we hadn't known her before.

Upon arrival that Friday afternoon, we had a blast playing ping pong, pool, and card games in the recreation room of the condo complex. We continued the fun that night in our condo with more games and a movie to watch.

We got up early on Saturday morning, and after

breakfast, headed to Heavenly Valley all bundled up. The boys looked really cute in their knit hats from Idaho! We rented skis for them and got them settled in their first lesson. When we saw that they were off to a good start, we headed up the mountain to get in a little skiing with Mills and Mayra. Michelle was also in a lesson. At lunchtime, we stopped early so "mama" could go to the bunny slope and take a few pictures. Their beautiful, black skin was such a contrast to the glistening white snow! The grins on their faces were brighter than we had seen them yet! Both were doing really well.

After lunch, we went with the boys to the practice hill for the rest of the afternoon. It was a challenge for them to get off of the chair lift! They fell more than once, but got themselves up. We skied down the hill with them, helping them with their turns. They had plenty of spills, but would giggle, get up, and go for more. By the end of the afternoon, they were both gliding down the hill, quite well for their first time. They told us that skiing was fun. We would definitely do some more of it with them.

Sephy (who doesn't ski) had fixed a nice dinner for us, and we were more than ready for it when we arrived back at the condo. The boys really enjoyed Michelle and Mayra's company that weekend, and all of us had such a great time.

The next morning, we headed out fairly early, since it had started snowing. We had to get home at a decent time because our son Craig, and his family were on their way to our house. They were also bringing Bruce's parents with them. We were celebrating Christmas early with them this year.

It was pouring rain in Watsonville, as our family arrived. We had a short visit that evening, and the next morning, we would celebrate our Christmas. We have a tradition of placing a bell on the table, so that the first one up can ring it and wake everyone up. Bruce's mom was the first up, but she didn't bother to ring the bell until the coffee was on. We had our traditional "Cheese Puff" for breakfast. It had been served at our morning wedding reception many years ago, and was now expected by our children on holidays. It's nice, because you can make most of it ahead, and then let it bake while we open the stocking stuffers.

Paul and Joseph really enjoyed their new nieces and nephews, and it was fun to watch them open their gifts. Of course, the boys enjoyed the big game set that they were given and the diaries and nice, warm long-sleeved shirts that Bruces' folks had brought along. We enjoyed their company that day, and I served the traditional raviolis that we have on special occasions before they left for home. The holiday spirit was definitely with us, even though Christmas was still six days away.

Merry Christmas

Chapter 10

After our family left, we continued our preparations for the holiday. On Wednesday of that week, we invited Debra Leigh over for brunch as a special way of thanking her for her generosity and investment into the boys' lives. Of course, there were cookies to bake, gifts to wrap, as well as Bruce and the boys sneaking around hiding things from me.

Thursday evening was a special time! The youth group at church was going Christmas caroling, and they would be coming over afterward for sloppy joes, hot chocolate and cookies. In addition, that night my "name sake niece" — Susie Jo and her husband Don Granner — were flying in from Michigan to spend the Christmas holiday with us. Bruce and I left for the airport with about 25 youth and the leaders still at our house. It was raining, and the Oakland airport was super busy. Since they had flown across country after working all day, they were hungry. It was now about 11:30 pm. We stopped for an "In-n-Out" burger as we drove back toward home. We heard a cell phone ringing. After realizing that it was Bruce's, he answered to Joseph's voice on the line. He said, "The party is over now." It was about midnight, and the guests had left. He wanted us to know that all was well.

Susie Jo and I went shopping the next day, as I had some gifts to purchase so I could fill the gigantic stockings I had bought for the boys. We spent the entire evening in my bedroom wrapping gifts and visiting. As much as I wanted to protect the boys from all the materialism in America, I found myself wanting to make up for all the things they never had. In retrospect, I think went a bit overboard for their first Christmas.

Early on in the Christmas season, they heard songs about and saw many Santa Clauses. This fat man with the red suit was entirely new to them. I explained that there had been a generous man in the days of old, named Saint Nicholas who had done good deeds for others. Then of course, I got out our book of 'Twas the Night Before Christmas, so they could know more about him. We had lots of fun singing "Santa Claus is Coming to Town", as we drove around town looking at all the Christmas lights.

The day before Christmas found me busy in the kitchen, again. There were more raviolis to make, as well as stuffed manicotti, and all the trimmings for our traditional Christmas Eve dinner. We had a custom of inviting some of our friends over whose families lived out of state. So, besides Susie Jo and Don, our good friends and former next-door neighbors, Bob and Julie Woolley, joined us. They brought over a Sudoku game for the boys, and after dessert, they taught us all how to play it. It was a wonderful evening, and the boys both seemed to enjoy it. The evening was rather long, however, for Bruce and Don. After the company left, they were out in the shop assembling a bicycle for Joseph and a basketball hoop and backboard for both of the boys. I think they actually saw Christmas day in by the time they were finished! Before bed, we placed the bell on the table, so that whoever was up first could ring in the holiday.

I guess my excitement for the first Christmas with our two new sons was responsible for me being the bell-ringer. Sleepily, everyone got up into the living room while I made hot chocolate and hot cider for everyone. I warmed up the oven to bake our traditional Christmas breakfast—cheese puff. As it was baking, we opened our gifts. Before we all sat down, we sent Joseph out to the garage for "something". There on the porch was a new bicycle. When he realized that it was for him, he came in with a big grin on his face and said, "Santa Clause came to town!" We then got both of them to look out front, where they saw the basketball hoop. Paul had an ear-to-ear smile as he opened up his very own new guitar.

We enjoyed our breakfast and then headed for church. I was particularly happy that their first American Christmas fell on a Sunday, so that part of this day would really honor the Lord and focus on the true meaning of the Christmas holiday. By the time we were home, it was raining once again. We all enjoyed the fire and the snowman jigsaw puzzle that we were putting together. Meanwhile, Bruce cooked the prime rib dinner with his incredible twice-baked potatoes. This momentous day went all too fast! My niece and her husband expressed how much it meant to them to be here with the boys on their first American Christmas.

When we asked the boys about Christmas in Sudan, they shared how the whole village would go to church on Christmas Eve and worship into the early morning hours. On Christmas morning, the first reveler who was awake would start the Christmas celebration by running house to house, each time picking up more neighbors. When the entire village was gathered, they would assemble for games and contests and dancing. Their rudimentary games played with sticks and stones didn't have to be purchased in a store. They were, non-the-less, fun and engaging for everyone. These fond memories they shared lit up their faces and warmed our hearts. We could tell that, despite all of the material blessings that we had bestowed upon them, their hearts were—in a large way—back in Africa. Bruce and I committed, right then and there, to do all in our power to help them retain their cultural values. These are values we see as far more important than material things.

San Francisco

Chapter 11

Bruce's company owns an apartment in the City, which overlooks the Embarcadero. This was available to the owners if there were no meetings taking place there. We had stayed there on several occasions—one of which was when Susie Jo and Don had come out for Thanksgiving a few years prior. Susie really likes the City, so we had surprised her with a two-night stay. I realized with Bruce retiring on January first, this would be our last chance to enjoy this fabulous amenity. So, the day after Christmas, we took off for San Francisco. The boys hadn't spent any time in a large American city, other than San Jose. We were anxious to show them the sights.

It so happens that this apartment is on the 14th floor of a rather unpretentious building. However, when you walk into the apartment, the million-dollar view takes your breath away! It is fantastic—Coit Tower, the Embarcadero Center, and the Bay Bridge all within eye-shot! Joseph bravely advanced out to the patio, only to grab the rail. He looked down and retreated backwards in fear. He wouldn't go near the railing the rest of the stay. I'll admit, it takes all of my courage to go out there, too.

The boys were awestruck as we took in the sights during the next few days. For two boys from a third world country where the tallest buildings were their one story mud huts; the high rise buildings that surrounded them were almost more than they could comprehend. Nevertheless, they seemed to be truly enjoying their first experience in a cosmopolitan city. Their comments spanned the spectrum from "there's so much noise I couldn't sleep the first night" to "the excitement of all that was going on is thrilling for people our age!" We took in Union Square (with the big, beautiful Christmas tree), the large tree at Neiman Marcus, Chinatown, Pier 39, Ghiradelli Square and Fisherman's Wharf. The weather was really beautiful. The after-Christmas sales, sights, smells and sounds of San Francisco were certainly luring their affections.

The last morning, we decided to take the elevator up to the top floor of the apartment building (about 24 floors, altogether). On top, was a beautiful patio with artificial turf, lounging chairs, and plants. The fear of heights was over. Joseph said that he wanted to sleep up there.

After a couple of wonderful days, it was time to head home. Tony and Lili were back from spending Christmas in Mexico City with her family. We were getting together with them the next evening, so that they could visit with Susie Jo and Don. Also, the next day, our "honorary" children would be arriving—Robb and Anna Huffman and their little boy, J.J. Anna had been my teacher's aid and then my student teacher. We were really fond of each other, so I sort of adopted her as my "ornery honorary daughter". We were thrilled when she married a young man that she had known in high school. We had grown fond of him from the first time we met him. They had recently moved to Pioneer— up in the Sierra Mountains. It had been a tradition to spend New Years Eve with them, so they arrived for that last weekend of 2005. We all brought in the New Year together. Little (18 month-old) J.J. really enjoyed the boys' attention! Many times that weekend when they were in their room—doing their own thing—he would walk in and demand their attention. They would stop what they were doing to crawl around on their hands and knees to play with him. We are so amazed at their natural and loving way with children. They are both like "kid magnets."

Happy New Year
Chapter 12

The holidays were now in the past, and life settled down to a more normal pace. We were back in our routine of the gym, home school, guitar lessons, youth group, as well as the visits with our social workers.

In early February, we were invited to join Mills & Sephy at Lake Tahoe once again. We had a great time, as usual. However, on Saturday when we planned to ski, the weather wasn't cooperative whatsoever. There was a combination of rain and snow coming down. We stood at the base of Heavenly Valley deciding if it was a good idea to buy our lift tickets, when it came down even harder!

An indoor sport seemed much more appropriate that day. Bowling fit the bill quite nicely. Of course, it was the first time for the boys, and they seemed to enjoy it a lot. We had a few laughs when Paul let the ball go the wrong way, and we all scattered from behind him. They also enjoyed their time with Mayra—who had been one of the most friendly and welcoming to them in the youth group. The pool table and ping pong tables at the condo were great fun again, especially since the boys were getting better at playing both of these games. That evening, we played many games of UNO, which is a big hit with them.

On Sunday, we drove down the mountain toward Pioneer. This just happened to be Super Bowl Sunday, and Robb and Anna had invited us to come and spend the day and night there. J.J. was so happy to see Paul and Joseph again! We had a wonderfully relaxing visit, and they had prepared a delicious spread of food to eat as we watched the game. Both of the boys expressed earlier that they didn't want to ever play American football. Their football—which is soccer—rules in their opinion. It certainly is not nearly as brutal! They surely seemed amused with all the hype over Super Bowl Sunday. Of course, a few more games of UNO were in order that evening.

The next morning, we headed to Twain Harte to visit with a long-time friend, Dan Shurr. We hadn't as yet seen his home in the mountains. It turned out to be a really great visit. The boys had fun challenging us to many games of pool down in his basement. We spent the night there, and early the next morning, Dan joined us at Dodge Ridge to ski. We bought the boys another lesson to make sure that they were comfortable. That afternoon, we skied down a really nice intermediate run. Both Joseph and Paul did really well. By now, they had mastered the art of getting off the chair lift without falling. Once again, they had big smiles on their faces as they skied along side of us.

After dropping Dan off back at his home, we headed back to Watsonville. In the car we had a multiplication marathon, as both boys were mastering the times tables.

In a few weeks, we would be celebrating President's weekend. I was ready for a "grandma fix"! Knowing the grand kids would have a few days off of school, we took the Hubbards up on their offer to let us use the mobile home in Pismo Beach that belongs to her folks. We picked up the three younger ones—Amber, Dominic, and Kaitlin. It rained quite a lot that weekend, but there were no dampened spirits at all. We played lots of UNO, ate pizza, watched videos, worked puzzles, and played on the beach between raindrops. Little Kaitlin talked and talked to Joseph. She would hardly leave him alone. Paul, Dominic, Amber and I were vying for the title of UNO champ. We took a break to attend church on Sunday morning, where the son-in-law of some of our friends preaches. The rest of the weekend was fun and games. As we dropped the grand kids off on Monday morning, Joseph, who had patiently listened to Kaitlin's constant chatter all weekend was to be admonished. "Joseph, you talk too much!" scolded Kaitlin. We all roared.

The boys were fitting into our home nicely, and we were so pleased that we had obeyed God's call. What a huge blessing we would have lost out on if we hadn't taken a risk and opened our hearts and home. They were working hard and learning a lot. Life was good!

Challenges
Chapter 13

March was upon us, and I was preparing to depart on my trip to Romania to teach at the Eastern European Bible College. I lined up school work for Bruce to supervise the boy's schooling, and gathered my own lesson plans for the first year students. I was excited about going back, but also hesitant about leaving my three men. I would meet up with our friends, Dr. David and Gretchen Kast, in Budapest. They would be teaching the second and third year students. We had been close friends from church, but they had recently moved to San Marcos to be near their new grandson.

It was a great time for me, even though I missed my guys. My many wonderful Romanian friends went out of their way to care for me, especially since I was without my "better half". This particular group of students at EEBC were such eager learners, and inspired me greatly with the special call on their lives to serve the Lord! During the first week of my stay— the 8th of March—Romania celebrated "Women's Day." I was blessed with bouquets of flowers, chocolates, and was made to feel so special. I had to really step out of my comfort zone that evening, though, as I had been asked to preach the sermon to the ladies in the church. The place was packed, and the Lord had placed a message on my heart to share. My wonderful translator, Sanda, standing up there next to me helped take the "edge" off of my nervousness. The weather was unusually cold, and I walked to school several days in my snow boots.

Meanwhile, back at the farm, the boys were having a good time. Bruce took them up to Dodge Ridge again to get a bit more skiing in. During the middle weekend of my absence, a big storm came in, and our deck was actually covered in snow! (This only happens once in a great while on the California central coast). Joseph excitedly said, "We can ski in the morning!"

The two weeks went rapidly, and I found myself in the Munich Airport. I was anxiously waiting to board my plane to cross the ocean toward home. Unfortunately, the plane was broken, and we had to wait about eight hours for a part to be flown in. Then it took quite a bit of time to put into the plane. Obviously, I wasn't going to get home on Saturday, as planned. I arrived in Chicago very late on Saturday night and was "put up" in a hotel near the airport.

My three men drove right from church to the airport to pick me up on Sunday afternoon. Boy, was I happy to see them, and I think the feeling was mutual!

We no sooner arrived home, than Bruce (who looked pale) said, "I don't feel so good. I need to go lie down for awhile." This is highly unusual for him.

I had purposed to stay awake until bedtime, so I could start getting back on California time. I caught up on mail, unpacking, etc. and fed the boys before taking them to youth group. Still, Bruce barely budged. He didn't want anything to eat and was still horizontal when I went to bed rather early. I guess my jet lag caught up with me. My own bed felt so good, and I was out for the count! I never heard Bruce get up (which is highly unusual for me, a very light sleeper) to go into the bathroom. All I heard was a loud sound. I thought it was the wastebasket hitting the floor. By the time I was conscious, he was climbing back into bed saying, "I passed out in the bathroom." Under normal circumstances, I would have been on my feet in a flash, but my weary travels had caught up with me.

The next morning, Bruce still didn't look or feel well, not to mention that now he had a nasty gouge near his brow where he hit the sink when he passed out. He phoned the Dr's office, but there were no available appointments. (I'm not at all sure that he didn't think that he had the flu and would be better in a day or two, so he didn't insist on going). By Monday night, he still was feeling and looking sick. I did hear him get up at about 3:00 a.m. He was getting dressed and told me that he needed to go down to Walgreens (which stays open all night) to get something to ease his discomfort. I promptly got out of bed and insisted that he not drive—I would take him. After throwing some clothes on, we headed out of the driveway. I said, "Why don't

I take you to the emergency room at the hospital?" He didn't go for that idea, so I made a deal with him. I would drive him to the drugstore tonight on the condition that he let me take him into the doctor first thing the next morning. He must have really felt bad, since he agreed with me!

On Tuesday morning, I got the boys started on their math test. I told them that I would be back after Bruce saw the doctor. We arrived at the office around nine o'clock. When they saw what Bruce looked like, we were led into an examining room right away. After Dr. Weber examined him, he said that he would call ahead to the hospital because Bruce needed to have some tests. We drove right over to Watsonville hospital and never left until about six o'clock that evening. I, of course, called the boys to let them know and gave them lunch instructions and more assignments over the phone. At about three in the afternoon, we were still there waiting, so I called Corine. She went over and picked up the boys so that she could fix some dinner for us.

Finally, the results were made known to us. There was a tumor on his left kidney! I was a bit numb since this was a man who had never spent a day in the hospital (except by my side) since the day he was born. Sometime that afternoon, during shift change for the nurses in the emergency room, a friendly face peeked into our examining room. It was a nurse who volunteered at the Pregnancy Resource Center, Trish Mather. What a comfort it was to us when she came in and prayed with us!

Soon after, we were sent to a room upstairs and

An Amazing Trek

Fifty young boys set out across the wild bush country between the White Nile and the Blue Nile, facing not only thirst, hunger, wild animals, innumerable rivers, but Muslim extremists who would exterminate them on sight. They traveled 135 miles in 3 months, staying off the roads and away from the villages. They land in a UN Refuge Camp, but what then?

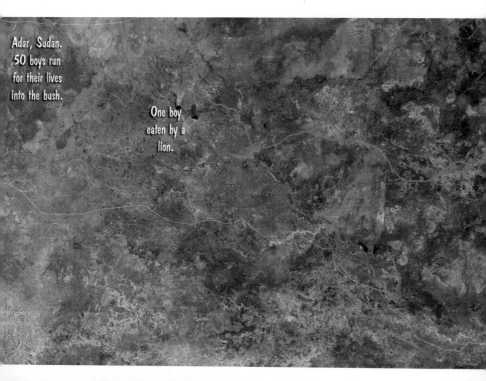

Adar, Sudan. 50 boys run for their lives into the bush.

One boy eaten by a lion.

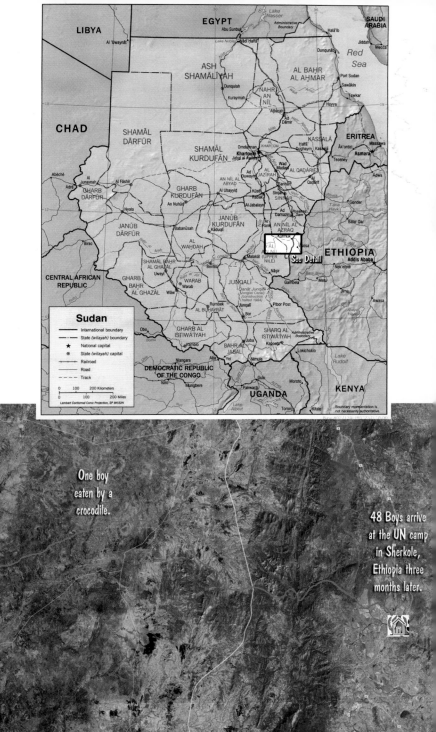

One boy eaten by a crocodile.

48 Boys arrive at the UN camp in Sherkole, Ethiopia three months later.

would wait there for Dr. Rosen (the surgeon) to come and speak with us. As soon as Bruce was settled, I phoned over to the church office to ask for prayer for him. A short time later, our associate pastor, Ray York, showed up. He had had a kidney removed about seven years earlier. As we were talking to Ray, in walked Dr. Rosen—the very same person who had operated on Ray! They were happy to see each other, and began chatting like long, lost friends. That brought us some more comfort just to see how our Lord, once again, orchestrates bringing certain people together in such circumstances. The good news was that in the years since Ray's surgery, the technique had been perfected and could be done laparoscopically—not the all-invasive type of surgery that Ray had undergone. The bad news was that his kidney would most likely need to be removed. Dr. Rosen explained that 90% of the time these tumors were cancerous, and that meant removing the whole organ. However, he wanted to do a few more tests and couldn't do the surgery until the next week, anyway. There was no sense for Bruce to remain in the hospital, so he got dressed and we headed to Dale & Corine's house to try and break the news to the boys.

The next few weeks were a merry-go-round of doctor's visits and tests. The first round of tests were inconclusive as to whether or not the tumor was cancerous. We had to go to the hospital for a biopsy, which ultimately showed that it was, indeed, cancerous. Surgery was set for a Tuesday morning, April third.

Meanwhile, I had a serious, heart-to-heart talk with my Lord. It went something like, "Lord, you know I can't do without this man—especially now with two boys to raise. Lord, you have to heal him!" I'm not usually so emphatic with Jesus (I do believe that His will is what's best for me), but I found myself pouring out my heart to Him. It was amazing the peace and strength I had through this entire ordeal. I truly felt His presence surround me, and I wasn't filled with worry and anxiety, which is too often my tendency. The Lord certainly helped me be strong for Bruce and the boys!

Plan A or Plan B? To Die or not to Die!
Chapter 14

During the few weeks that elapsed since we discovered the tumor, things had been a bit hectic. I could tell that the situation seemed to have taken a toll on the boys. They were not exactly "themselves", and that added a bit of strain in the home. Sister Marilyn had called one day to ask if she could come for a visit on Sunday, since she was speaking at a church in our area. I invited her for dinner with us after church. She'll probably never quite know what a help she was to us. She explained that in Sudan, if a person was going to the hospital, it was usually to die. In the back of their minds, Joseph and Paul were probably thinking that Bruce was headed for his literal deathbed! No wonder, they had been acting strangely—the man who was so good with them and to them—their new American dad was going to die!

A few nights later, our friends, Mike and Kathy Smith, who had moved up to Oregon stopped by while they were visiting in Watsonville. As we talked, they mentioned that they were present when Pastor Ray had come out of his surgery those years earlier.

They also mentioned that they couldn't believe how bad he looked when he came out of the recovery room. Right then and there, I decided that if Bruce looked that bad, I would not have Joseph and Paul come to see him!

The morning of April third came with more rain. We were up early to get Bruce to the hospital before 7:00. Debra Leigh was going to pick up the boys and keep them at school for the entire day. We heard a knock on the front door in the darkness of the early morning. There were the Hubbards—all four of them—up so early to pray with us. What a blessing to have such a "send-off"! As we pulled into the parking lot at the hospital, we were met by Pastor Dennis who also wanted to pray with us. He would go and get his daughter from swimming and be back after awhile.

Meanwhile, I had come up with Plan A or Plan B. Plan A was that if Bruce came out looking awful, Kellie Hubbard would feed the boys dinner and take them with her to church afterward to help fill food bags for the upcoming Easter food giveaway. If he looked good, then we'd go with Plan B—the Woolleys would pick up the boys and bring them up to the hospital.

After Bruce was prepped and taken into the surgery room, I went to the waiting room. It was such a blessing to have Julie Woolley, Corine, Ray and Judy York, and Pastor Dennis all there with me! They kept my mind occupied and gave me such comfort. There were also phone calls from other friends that I had to step outside (into the rain) to answer. Finally, after about four hours of waiting, the Doctor came out. He said that Bruce had done well, and that the cancer was contained on the left kidney. How grateful I was that the Lord had heard my prayers! The others left, and Julie, Corine, and I went to have lunch in the cafeteria. They left soon afterward, and I was told where I could go and sit to be there when they wheeled Bruce from the recovery room. I still didn't know if I would go with Plan A or Plan B.

Later that afternoon, I anxiously awaited the opening of the elevator door. They finally wheeled Bruce out, and much to my amazement (and relief), he looked really good! We got him settled into his room, so I called Julie Woolley to confirm that they would bring the boys up after dinner. Meanwhile, Bruce insisted on sitting up and walking some. He was able to take a phone call from our dear friend, Laurentiu, in Romania. Also, Craig, Francine, and the grandchildren all appeared a little while later. His spirits were really good, and he was doing remarkably well!

That evening, Joseph and Paul appeared at the door with Bob and Julie. They visited for a little while, and then left the boys there to ride home with me. Both boys showed signs of relief to see Bruce sitting up and walking around. We showed them around the hospital floor, and they both said, "This is a nice place."

Bruce was feeling quite well and begged the doctor to let him come home. So, late in the afternoon, the day after his surgery, he was released.

We got him home and settled in. Paul and I went to get his prescriptions filled, and Joseph stayed right there with Bruce. For the next few days, he had a bit of difficulty eating, but that only lasted for a short time. He was gaining strength each day. We sure enjoyed the visit from Glenn and Carol Finks who drove all the way from Coarsegold to see Bruce.

It was now the week before Easter. Our church was doing their wonderful musical performance the weekend of Palm Sunday. The boys wanted to attend, so they invited Debra Leigh to meet them there. I stayed with Bruce. They had a wonderful time, and actually helped out afterward to assist with feeding the homeless that had been brought in to have a meal and watch the presentation. I got to see the program on Sunday morning, when Bruce insisted that he could be left alone for a couple of hours.

His stomach finally settled down, and he continued to gain strength. He was looking forward to Easter, and it was his first time back to church since his surgery. Craig and his family came, and we had our good friend, Bruce Hinman, over. Also, Lili's sisters were all visiting from Mexico City, along with her three nieces. They came over, too, and we managed an Easter egg hunt after it stopped raining. It was a wonderful day, but Bruce was pretty tired when everyone left that evening. The boys seemed to really enjoy their first American Easter celebration.

More Challenges
Chapter 15

One of the things we had been taught in our training at Catholic Charities was that often times, the refugee young people would experience some struggles about six months after coming to America. By then, the newness and excitement of American living would wear off, and the realization that they would not be returning to their homeland would set in. They were right. As if classic textbook, shortly after Easter, Paul had a meltdown. He became pretty depressed and informed us that he wanted to go back to Africa. Of course, this wasn't a remote possibility for him, as it wasn't practical. The UN Camp in Sherkole wouldn't accept him back, and it wasn't safe to return to Sudan. Talk about a "Lost Boy"! Here he was in a country that he didn't feel was his, and the country that had been his was no longer a safe option.

My heart was breaking for him, and his was broken in two. He stayed in his room or walked around the farm looking so totally downcast. We could see Joseph talking to him, fairly emphatically, in Mabaan. But of course, we didn't understand a word of the exchange. We finally had a break in the rain, and I just had to get out of the heavy atmosphere around the house for a little while. I drove over to Pinto Lake on a sunny and gorgeous spring day, and walked around just praying for Paul. His attitude toward us was not friendly, and we could tell that he was going through such a difficult time. He wouldn't even go with us to Bonfante Gardens, a theme park in Gilroy. We had planned an outing since it was Easter break, and Bruce was feeling up to it.

Thank goodness for the support we had in the URM program. We placed phone calls to Terry Watters, our case worker from Adopt International, as well as our new case worker—Sister Kathleen Connelly—from Catholic Charities. (Teresa Samuel-Boko was now home tending to her newborn son). They both came down to talk to Paul. I had such respect for the way both of them handled things. Terry and Bruce asked Paul a lot of practical questions, such as, "Where would you fly to, and how would you get the money for the plane ticket? Who would pick you up at the airport? How would you get back to Sherkole?" Of course, in his highly emotional state, he hadn't considered the practicalities. He came to the conclusion that a return would not be possible.

Sister Kathleen took him out for a bite to eat, and came back to talk to us. She felt that the boys were not getting enough exposure to other young people, and that they needed more. They were to be enrolled in a regular school with everyday classes by summer. (Which was a goal we had for them, too). Also, she felt that they needed more physical activity. We enrolled them in Tae Kwon Do with the local Police Activities League. They enjoyed the lessons, which were held twice a week. We also found that they had soccer following Tae Kwon Do, which of course, was a must for the boys. They enjoyed it a lot, but unfortunately, the other boys and the coach spoke mostly in Spanish. One day, as I watched them play, I saw Paul—knocked to the ground on his seat—kick a goal from a sitting position!

In a short time, Paul was back to his old self, and I was so very grateful to see him smiling and laughing again. Early on during this dark time, I had told Paul that I was praying for him. It broke my heart to hear him say that I shouldn't pray for him because he didn't deserve it. How conflicted he must have been! I felt so badly that he was so down on himself that he didn't feel worthy of being prayed for! Both Bruce and I tried very hard to overlook the negative attitude and just continue to love him through it. We also didn't want to overlook our attention to Joseph, because we knew that he was also sad to see Paul hurting so much.

This had been, by far, the most challenging time for all of us. But, our Lord had been so faithful to give us strength and wisdom. Through all of the difficult circumstances that come our way, He can bring some good out of them. We were now feeling closer than ever as a family because we had—together—weathered the storm.

New Experiences

Chapter 16

At our small airport in Watsonville, there is a wonderful program called the Young Eagles. On the first Saturday of each month (as weather permits), pilots with their private airplanes donate their services to encourage young people to become interested in flying. The first Saturday in May dawned brightly, so we found ourselves out at the airport with the boys. The place was abuzz with excitement! As people arrive, parents fill out a permission form, and then the young people get chosen on a first-come, first-serve basis. We were some of the first there, so the boys were called right away to sit and receive the ground school instruction. A man explains the parts of an airplane and demonstrates on a model, how the parts work together to make the plane fly. Next, they are assigned to a pilot who takes them up for about a twenty-minute flight over the Monterey Bay. It was a hoot to watch Joseph, Paul, and the other boy (who happened to be the son of the nurse who had prayed with us in the hospital). What huge smiles were on their faces, as that plane taxied to the runway! Bruce and I enjoyed the beautiful morning watching the planes come and go, as we munched on the refreshments that the Young Eagle Program provides. After about a half-hour, we saw the tan and white plane taxiing back toward us. The boys disembarked from the plane, just beaming! Tom, the pilot, had actually let Joseph fly it a little. They had also taken some really beautiful pictures with our camera of the coast and the green agricultural fields from up above. A young lady (who they knew from their school) was taking Polaroid pictures of the boys with their pilot. They received the photo along with a Young Eagles Certificate. That proved to be a successful Saturday venture. We couldn't help but wonder if this changed their perspective about airplanes being used for a worthy purpose as opposed to the destruction that small planes had brought to their young life in the village.

Mother's Day came, and it was really special to celebrate with my two wonderful new sons. After church, I had the choice of activities, so I requested that we go hiking at the Pinnacles National Monument. I hadn't been there in many years, and after all of the rain we had been blessed with this year, I knew the wildflowers would be spectacular. That assumption proved to be true. In order to hike to the lake there, we had to crawl through the dark, damp caves. The afternoon was warm, but it proved to be a pleasant experience. On the way back through Hollister, we stopped over at Tony and Lili's home, where we had been invited for a delicious Mother's Day dinner.

Memorial Day weekend arrived. Each year, our

church sponsors a Father/Son camp-out at a ranch nearby, which is owned by the family of one of our members. Bruce thought that it would be nice to take the boys—especially since Little Bear Wheeler was going to be there with his son. Little Bear is a wonderful man who has a fantastic knowledge of many of the American heroes. He dresses up like one of the characters, such as Sgt. York of World War I, and does a monologue that makes you feel like you are right there. He had been to dinner at our home back in November when he visited our church, and he and the boys enjoyed meeting each other. It seemed as though there was a conflict, however. Our pastor's daughter, Devony, was having her 16th birthday party that night. As it turned out, Paul chose to go with Bruce to the camp-out, and Joseph chose to go to the party. He expressed that he didn't want to miss his chance to be there with all of the girls! (He had figured that many of the guys would be at the camp-out.)

On the Sunday of Memorial Day weekend, our church traditionally has a big celebration in the afternoon and evening. There are food booths, a baseball game, egg toss, tug-of-war, jumping house, etc. In the evening, there is a special patriotic program, where all the Veterans and servicemen and women are honored. The entire community is invited to attend, so it is fun to meet and greet the visitors. Then, as it becomes dark enough, a Fireworks Extravaganza is the much anticipated event. The boys had never seen fireworks, so I was really curious what they would think. They both jumped when the first one went off, but they truly enjoyed the beauty of the sky lighting up as the music played.

The school year was coming to a close. The boys were continuing to work hard on their English, and the teachers at Pacific Coast Charter School all seemed pleased with their progress. They enjoyed the field trips to the San Francisco Zoo, as well as to Henry Cowell Redwood Park. It was a wonderful moment for us when they received (along with Kelly McGuckin) the achievement awards at the graduation ceremony. It was a bit difficult to say good-bye to Debra Leigh and all the staff at the Pacific Coast Charter School. They had truly embraced the boys.

To celebrate the boys' achievement and to keep our promise to them, we headed up to the mountains two days after school got out. On Sunday evening, we stayed with the Finks' in Coarsegold, and Monday morning took off to Yosemite with our bikes. The waterfalls were truly spectacular, and we all enjoyed riding our bikes through Yosemite Valley. We picnicked by the Merced River. It was a picture perfect day, and fortunately, it wasn't too crowded.

The Good Ol' Summertime
Chapter 17

Shortly after school was out, we faced still another challenge with the boys. I was personally struggling. It seemed as though all of my time was spent in teaching the boys, driving them to school, Tae Kwan Do, etc. Oftentimes, in the car, they wouldn't talk—just sit quietly. One morning, when Bruce had taken me on our Saturday breakfast date, I found myself in tears—right there in the restaurant. I told him that I sometimes felt like a cook, taxi driver, and household slave. I so desired to have that bonding with the boys, but it didn't seem to be progressing—at least not to the degree that I longed for. I was so conflicted inside! I really wanted to serve the Lord and them unselfishly—expecting nothing in return. However, I also longed to have a close relationship. Bruce committed to talking to the boys, which he did.

The next day, I prepared our Sunday dinner while the three guys were out in the shop. Bruce made it a point to thank me for the wonderful meal in front of the boys as an example for them, hoping they would follow suite. As I was cleaning up the kitchen, he asked them to come and thank me. They looked at each other, concluded that that wouldn't happen, and refused. At that point, Bruce told the boys that they really needed to say thank you because it would help them in life. And, more important, it was the right thing to do. Ever the leader, Bruce told them that in America, appreciation is appropriate when someone does something nice for you. In our home, it was expected. Still, they wouldn't say thanks. Later that afternoon, the boys came dressed for their youth group meeting, expecting Bruce to give them a ride (which he normally did). Bruce told them that if they couldn't say thanks, he couldn't give them a ride. The atmosphere around the house was getting thick again. When they still wouldn't say thank you by the next day, Bruce decided that he had to really make his point. So, he stepped up the consequences of their choice. They would be required to make their own meals until they could say thank you when someone else did it for them. When they still refused a thanks, he decided to escalate the consequences yet another step. Bruce explained that there are rules in our home that need to be followed, unless they could show him a really good reason why they shouldn't be. So, if they couldn't figure out how to say thank you by Tuesday morning, he would take their cell phones away. For every day they refused a thank you, he would keep their phones for a month. These phones were so important to the boys, because they were able to call their friends from Sudan who had settled in other parts of the U.S. — Philadelphia,

Boston, Nebraska, Nevada, Texas, and Washington. We had gotten a plan that gave free calling on the weekends, and they really enjoyed talking to their friends (in Mabaan). Tuesday morning, they were either to surrender their phones or say thank you. When Bruce went in to see what they had decided to do, he was handed a thank you/apology note from each boy. They both came to me to say thank you and express their appreciation for all we had done for them. They were sorry for being so stubborn and expressed that they didn't know why they had acted so badly. Of course, I gave them a hug and told them they were forgiven.

Some time later, I was invited to hear a missionary from Africa speak at a Women of Vision gathering. She shared that in Africa, the men sit and talk and have meetings all day. The women gathered the water and wood, worked in the fields, and did all the housekeeping chores. Suddenly it dawned on me—it wasn't about me personally! We had been having a cultural clash at our home. Fortunately, we had weathered another storm, and the boys now express their gratitude freely. In fact, now, all three of them ban me from the kitchen on Sundays and take over all of the cooking duties!

I gained even further insight into the relationship between African boys and their mothers when we were being interviewed by a man from public radio. He was doing a radio program about the unaccompanied refugee minors and asked to come to our home to interview us. By this time, the boys were doing so much better on their English skills that they consented. It was an eye-opener for me! Joseph shared with the man that in Sudan when they were six or seven, their fathers discouraged them from hanging around their mothers. They were called the equivalent of sissy if they were seen with their moms. They were to hang out with the men. With a concept like that ingrained in them at such a young age, no wonder they didn't talk much to me. Also, now they were at an age when they were considered men, and their mother had to drive them where they wanted to go! No wonder they sat so quietly in the car!

Meanwhile, we were working hard to come up with a plan for their schooling. We lived about five minutes from a wonderful school—Monte Vista Christian School—and our heart's desire was for the boys to be able to attend there. Our son, Craig, had graduated from there some years ago, and I had been working as a substitute teacher there for about eight years prior to the boys' arrival. The school has a reputation for being college prep, and for expecting a lot from the students. In addition, they have a boarding program for foreign students. They have young people from Korea, Taiwan, Japan, Hong Kong, and other countries. We felt that this would be a good fit for the boys. I always enjoyed my time out there as a substitute teacher—the atmosphere was wonderful, and the students were a lot of fun to be around. For me, it had been such a positive experience because most of my former students went on to attend Monte Vista. It was fun to see them mature and to attend their graduations.

From the day the boys arrived, I began praying that they could attend Monte Vista.

Bruce and I made an appointment to take the boys there and talk to the Superintendent, Steve Sharp. He was so warm and encouraging, and was positive about the boys being able to attend. We decided to start them out as Freshmen, due to the large gap in their education. We completed the application process, and they were accepted.

That left us with some choices to make about summer school. We had applied to Cabrillo College for the boys to take some ESL (English as a Second Language) classes there. We had even ridden the bus with them so that they would be familiar with the transportation system. We felt badly, however, that they would have to miss Donnie Moore Youth Camp, which was scheduled during classes. We were aware that Monte Vista had a six-week ESL summer program for the incoming foreign students, but didn't realize that it was a possibility for the boys. One day, Martha Price—whose in-laws were the founders of Monte Vista back in 1926—called on the phone to say that they were inviting the boys to attend. We would have to pay for the field trips, which we were most happy to do. They would still have to miss Youth Camp, but what a great opportunity to get to know the school and the incoming foreign students.

This class wouldn't start until after the 4th of July, so we decided that a trip to Disneyland would offer the boys a great experience. We left early one morning and stopped in Nipomo to pick up

Amber, Dominic, and Kaitlin. At full capacity, our van arrived before noon in Anaheim. We stopped at our hotel to check in and pick up some slightly discounted tickets. We walked on over to California Adventure. Obviously, this was a whole new world for two boys from Sudan. Our favorite attraction there was "Soaring over California," though the boys were captivated by the parade. They seemed to really enjoy the music and dancing.

Early the next morning, we arrived at Disneyland. Since we were some of the first into the park, we were able to walk right in line for the Matterhorn, and Small World. Soon, though, the place became packed and the lines were long. It was really warm that day, too. One of the most memorable experiences was "Honey, I Shrunk the Kids." In the theatre, with 3-D glasses, the dog becomes really big and sneezes into the audience. Just at that moment a misty spray is released from somewhere near your face. When the mouse goes into the machine on stage, suddenly hundreds of mice come out—as if into the audience—and you feel a sensation of mice running up your leg. (Though I know it isn't real, I've never quite made it through that part without screaming.)

Some time later, the boys were asked to write an essay about their favorite trip for a class assignment. Bruce was helping Paul write about Disneyland and when he mentioned "Honey, I Shrunk the Kids", Paul said, "Oh no. I didn't like those mice running up my leg!" Bruce explained to him that it wasn't real, and Paul protested, "But I felt them." We were horrified that all this time he thought his new parents would take him someplace where mice attacked you! It was the beginning of an awareness on our part, that the boys had been in such survival mode, that imagination was a foreign concept to them. The next day, Bruce snuck up behind Joseph and pretended to sneeze as he squirted some water from a squirt bottle on him. He also did this to Paul. They laughed when they realized it was a squirt bottle, and were beginning to understand a bit about imagination.

After a full day and night at Disneyland, where the boys—again—enjoyed the Electric Light Parade, we spent a couple of hours the next day at Newport Beach. We wanted them to experience swimming in the ocean where it wasn't as cold as it is up in Santa Cruz County. Our grandkids had a good time, and they totally enjoyed being around Paul and Joseph.

Soon, it was the 4th of July. They understood from our studies in American history why we were celebrating, and I wanted them to experience some of the local flavor. That afternoon, we headed for downtown Watsonville to see the 4th of July parade. I think they enjoyed it, and we saw several people that we knew—both in the parade, as well as spectators. That evening, the Miracle family and Cal and Julia Hicks came over for a bar-b-que. We ended up watching fireworks from our deck that night, as several of the displays in the area lit up the night sky.

Their first day of ESL at Monte Vista rolled around. It turned out that one of the three teachers for the summer program was Joe McCroskey, a really great guy that I had known for several years. We often ate lunch together when I was substituting, and I had been praying for his family to be chosen for some of the new housing in Watsonville. Our prayers were answered, and I had attended the joyous housewarming celebration the winter before. His fellow teachers were Beth Livingston and Shari McQueen. The students worked in the computer lab, as well as in the classroom. Every week, there was a fieldtrip. They got to go to San Francisco and Angel Island, San Luis Obispo to visit Cal Poly and see Hearst Castle—to name a few of the destinations. These would involve an overnight stay in a hotel, meals at restaurants, and lots of interesting sights. On the menu at one of their lunches out, Paul saw an entrée of "chicken fingers." Though he really likes chicken, he thought that they were serving chickens' claws (which didn't appeal to him in the least)! Only when someone else had ordered it, and he saw what they were, did he realize that he had missed out on something really good. We all got a laugh over his "chicken fingers" story. What a wonderful time the boys had for those six weeks!

There were also some local fieldtrips. Joe had asked if we would like to accompany them to Gizdich Ranch—a nearby attraction—where people can go to pick their own berries and eat some of the good pies that they make in the bake shop there. All of us got a laugh out of the fact there here we were picking strawberries there, when we had acres of them in our front yard! It was fun for me to become acquainted with some of their classmates. The boys were sure progressing with their English.

They took a few days off from the summer class because Catholic Charities had enrolled them in soccer camp at Santa Clara University. The timing was great, because the field trip that week was a visit to Santa Clara. The boys didn't miss out too much—in fact, they had a fantastic time at the camp. They stayed in the dorm and received really good instruction in soccer. It was particularly hot that week, but that didn't dampen their enthusiasm. After their first day there, Bruce and I received a call that night from Joseph. He asked us to bring him a new pair of soccer shoes. Bruce asked him what happened to his, and he said, "they really stink!" After holding back his laughter, Bruce told him that he needed to put them on the windowsill and air them out. We didn't replace shoes because of their smell, and, besides, it was too late to buy new ones anyway.

It so happened that this summer was our 30th anniversary. Bruce surprised me with a cruise to Alaska—something I had wanted to do for a long time. Sister Kathleen volunteered to come and stay with the boys for that week. We had a marvelous time, but found ourselves calling home about every other day. The boys enjoyed their time with this wonderful, fun-loving lady. They grilled steaks for her one night, and as she put it, "They took good care of me." One evening during our trip, the boys took Debra Leigh to a production of Guys and Dolls at Cabrillo College. This was their gift to her at the end of the year. They also escorted Sister Kathleen to a classic car show at Monte Vista during our absence. All four of us had a good time, but we were sure happy to see each other at the end of the week!

We were blessed that first summer with some wonderful guests in our home. Our dear friends from Romania—Adi and Flori Galiger—came to stay for a week in June. They really enjoyed getting to know the boys. We had fun playing games, taking them to the Santa Cruz Beach Boardwalk, and up into the mountains to see Camp Harmon (the Easter Seals camp for handicapped children). This camp is near and dear to our heart since Bruce is the Board Chairman for Easter Seals of Central California.

In August, we were blessed with a visit from the Peter Ministr family from Prague. Peter is the Director of Teen Challenge in Eastern Europe, and we had been there to help renovate a building on one of our mission trips. This was the first time that he was able to bring his whole family with him—his wife, Patricia, and his three teenage children. It was amazing to see how fast these five teenagers from such different parts of the world bonded during that week! They had much fun playing UNO, basketball, and riding the rides at the Boardwalk. There were tears in all of our eyes when we had to say good-bye.

All too fast, summer was drawing to a close. The ESL class ended. Joe McCroskey and his family, along with Beth Livingston and her escort picked up the boys one evening and drove up to San Jose to take them to dinner at an Ethiopian restaurant. Both of the boys enjoyed eating some of the familiar cuisine. They brought home a doggy box so that we could taste. I must say, there was a spice of some kind that was way too hot for my taste buds!

The week before school started, we decided that we would paint the boys' room and really get it organized. It was a family project that lasted a couple of days. We learned that they are both pack rats. It was amazing the things that we found accumulating in their desk drawers in just 10 months! Of course, we also did some school shopping. They were already growing out of some of the clothes we had bought when they came.

The last weekend of August, our church choir was taking their annual trip to do an outreach at the San Francisco Rescue Mission in the Tenderloin District. Bruce and I felt that we wanted the boys to experience some giving back of their lives to those less fortunate. There were many jobs to be done there, which made use of people with talents other than singing. We all found ourselves working really hard in the kitchen—making huge pots of spaghetti sauce, and boxing up meals for about 600 people. In addition, we had to help with meals for the hundred or so people from our church. Though we worked hard, it felt good to be serving others—alongside our boys.

A Miracle Named Karen

Chapter 18

Monday morning dawned brightly, and there was excitement in the air! It was the first day for the boys to attend regular high school at Monte Vista Christian. We had gone the week before to get their schedules and locate all their classrooms, buy gym clothes, and make sure that their locker combinations worked well. We wanted that first day to be as comfortable as possible for them.

They came home all smiles, and they seemed really happy to be there. Joe McCroskey, (who had been a Spanish teacher there for many years) had been convinced to teach the ESL Classes this year. They really love this man, and he loves his students! They would have three of their classes with him, including Bible. In addition, they both had beginning orchestra, PE, Algebra, Photography (Joseph), and Auto Mechanics (Paul).

That night, we asked if they needed some help on their homework. Out came this big, thick Algebra book. I never understood Algebra the first time around, barely passing. In fact, I cried many tears over all of the math I had taken in school! Just the sight of this book intimidated me. Bruce had to leave for a meeting at church, and I gulped at the thought of assisting them. I would definitely need the Lord's help for this task! We began, and the first part wasn't so bad. It was a review of some basic math. Also, I discovered that some of the answers were in the back of the book. We could do this! Two hours later, Bruce came home; and we were still working. Half way through the second page, I was stuck. He looked at it, and said, "I sure don't remember this." We finally muddled through, after about three hours.

I went to bed, quite exhausted and discouraged. I just couldn't face a whole year of three hours per night on one subject. I awoke early the next morning, still feeling tired. I cried out to the Lord, "PLEASE help me. This is more than I can do!"

After the boys got off to school, I went to my aerobics class. I really needed to work out all the stress I was feeling. Most of the time, I take the class and come home in my sweaty clothes. After my housework, I take a shower. This particular day, I had some errands to run, so I took my clothes and would shower at the Spa. After class, I was in the locker room when I saw a lady that I hadn't seen in quite awhile. Her name is Karen Barton. I had taught her daughter some years before, and we had seen each other occasionally since then. One time, I saw her at the Mall, and we decided to have at bite to eat so that we could visit. This morning, we began to chat. I asked her about her daughter, Monica, and then filled her in on our life with the boys. I happened to mention that I was feeling panicked this particular morning due to the "battle of the Algebra book" the night before. She looked at me with much compassion and said, "You know, I was teaching Algebra at San Benito High School (which I had known, but forgotten). I am actually out on a leave, and I would be willing to tutor your boys." I stood there in awe! God had answered my prayer, and in such a marvelous and immediate way! We exchanged phone numbers, and I felt like I was floating as I left the spa. The amazing thing is that to this day, I've never seen her in the Spa again.

The boys began their tutoring twice a week, and I felt great relief. Karen is such a beautiful Christian woman! She prayed for the boys, encouraged them with scripture, provided them with snacks, and generally loved them into learning Unfortunately, their grades in Algebra were still not good after about a month of tutoring. I didn't want them to become discouraged, so I e-mailed the two different Algebra teachers and asked for a meeting. As we sat down, I was introduced to the head of the math department. She was so humble and apologetic. She explained to me that all of the ESL students had taken a Math placement test that summer (which I was unaware of.) Joseph and Paul, due to their fifth grade education, obviously hadn't done too well. They should have been placed in the Resource Math Class, but somehow they had slipped trough the cracks. In the Resource Class, they would have the same material, but at a slower pace. Algebra I would be taught as IA the first year and IB the second year. This special class was taught by a really encouraging teacher, Greg Davis, and there were only about eight students in it. This was perfect for Paul and Joseph. We had to do some changes in their schedule. It meant that Paul had to drop out of orchestra and replace it with a Study Hall to fit into the time slot for Algebra. He wasn't at all upset by this, so it worked out well. By the end of the first grading period, they both had an A in Algebra.

Autumn "Leaves"
Chapter 19

Right after Labor Day, Bruce was preparing to leave for Romania and Prague. He was leading a group from the church to help finish the remodeling of the new building that the Eastern European Bible College had purchased. Then, the second week, they would travel to Prague to help Peter Ministr work on the remodel of their new facility outside of the city. I would be both Mom and Dad for a few weeks.

Back-to-School Night was that week, and I ran back and forth between both boys' classes to meet all of their teachers. Of course, I was the sole homework helper. This was a real stretch the night Paul asked me to help him with his Auto Mechanics. I am probably the most unmechanical woman this side of the Mississippi (if not the entire U.S.)! As we were half way through the assignment, the phone rang. It was Bruce calling from Romania (the next morning, there); and we both had a good laugh when I told him what I was doing. Actually, it was a fun challenge to learn a little about cams and push rods!

The next weekend, the Santa Cruz County Fair was in full swing. Our neighbor, Katie Hubbard, had been raising a pig. The boys had been the official twice-a-day pig feeders whenever Katie had gone out of town. On Saturday morning, the Junior Livestock Auction took place, and she wanted the boys to come and watch her pig get auctioned off. It is a lively affair with the audience shaking taped-up soda cans filled with beans to encourage people to bid higher. Several of their friends from the Youth Group were also auctioning off their animals, so it turned out to be an exciting experience for them.

We had one extra ticket to the Fair, and when I asked the boys who they would like to invite along, Paul (without any hesitation) said, "Devony." This wonderful young lady—our pastor's daughter—was new at Monte Vista, too. She had been home schooled for most of her education, and was now a Junior. She was such a good friend to the boys, and they were really fond of her. She met us out there, and we spent most of the day looking at all the interesting exhibits. Several people stopped to talk to the boys and find out where they were from. It was a great day for celebrating God's gracious bounty.

Thankfully, Bruce returned home on schedule. We were all ecstatic to have him home again! I'll admit, I was relieved to have help driving the boys back and forth to their activities.

Joseph's one-year anniversary came, and we had decided to celebrate their birthdays on their arrival date. We took him to a restaurant of his choice (Outback Steakhouse). He beamed as the waiters sang Happy Birthday to him and came with a chocolate sundae topped with a lit candle. After dinner he picked out a new cell phone as his birthday gift.

Homecoming was early this year—the end of September. Mr. McCroskey had assigned all of his ESL students to help on their class's floats. That Friday when I picked up the boys from school, Paul told me that he was asked to ride on the Freshman float at half-time. We got him there early, so he could report to the parade staging area. The float happened to have a "Star Wars" theme, and there he was—all dressed in a white robe. He certainly stood out with that huge white smile to match that robe! After the game, they attended their first ever high school dance—a sock hop. They came home all smiles. While waiting for a call to pick them up, Bruce and I chuckled as we thought about two senior citizens having to stay up late in our role as chauffeurs.

Before we knew it, November had arrived. The boys were really doing well and were thriving at school. It was time to celebrate Paul's birthday. He chose to have a few of his friends (who lived in the dorm) over on Friday evening. After we ate, we all went to the Monte Vista football game. Afterward, we came back for some quick cake and ice cream before the boys had to be checked back in at the dorm.

On Saturday, (the official anniversary of his first year) Joe Mc Croskey called in the morning (as Paul had told me he would). He asked if I could help chaperone several of the students at the airport for the Young Eagles program. It was a glorious, sunny autumn day, and the students really enjoyed flying over the Bay in the private planes. That evening, Tony and Lili came to help us celebrate. Ever the thrifty one, Paul wanted dinner at home. I fixed the meal of his choice—roast chicken, with all the trimmings. Of course, we had fun playing some serious UNO afterward. We couldn't believe how fast the first year with the boys had flown!

Happy Holidays
Chapter 20

The holidays came around again, and this year, both of the boys and their families came for Thanksgiving. The weather was unusually warm, so there were many games of ping-pong out on the back porch, along with lots of other activity. We kept our tradition of sharing our gratefulness around the table. My heart was full of praise to our Lord for these precious young men that He had sent our way to complete our family.

A month or so earlier, as I sat in church one Sunday, I was reflecting on my life. As a young girl, I had dreamed of marrying and having five children. Unfortunately, after the birth of my first—Kylee—I had endometriosis and was unable to have more children. Four years after my divorce, I had married Bruce who had sole custody of Anthony and Craig. I instantly became the mother of three, much to my delight. Suddenly, that morning at church—it dawned on me. The Lord had—once again—granted me the desires of my heart! One of the verses I had claimed was Psalm 37:4—"Delight yourself in the Lord and He will give you the desires of your heart." With the coming of Joseph and Paul, I was the mother of five. I never would have dreamed that two of them would be sent to me from Africa!

We had a wonderful time playing games and working puzzles as we ate our pie that evening. Craig's family spent the night, so we got to enjoy them for most of the next day, too.

During Thanksgiving weekend, we had an important job to do. By this time, Lili was six months pregnant for her and Tony's first child. We had purchased a crib as a gift for the baby, and it needed to be assembled. The boys worked alongside of Bruce and Tony. All four of my men were so proud of the job they had done!

The weeks between Thanksgiving and Christmas flew by, as usual. On the last day of school, 2006, there was a fieldtrip with the ESL students. Joe had asked if we would go along to chaperone and transport some of the students. We took a tour of Long Marine Lab in Santa Cruz and went to the Natural Bridges State Park to see the butterflies that migrate here each year. (We had lived in the area since 1986 and had never visited either one of these). It was a wonderful way to bring in the Christmas break.

The holidays were full of entertaining opportunities. We had Joe McCroskey and his family over for dinner one evening, as well as Debra Leigh and Kelly McGuckin for a holiday breakfast. Bruce's mom came to stay for a few days. His Dad had passed away that October, and she was pretty lonely. (They had been married for 62 years). We all felt it would help her to get away for a short time. The boys enjoyed learning to play Skip-Bo, her favorite game.

The Saturday before Christmas, we were hosting the Bruscia family party. Mom would get a ride back home with Bruce's sister, Donna, and her husband, Leonard. Mom kept me company as I stood for about three hours making raviolis for everyone. It was a great celebration, as we don't often get together with Bruce's nieces and their families. Of course, our two boys and their families came, too.

We departed from tradition a bit this year. We had our raviolis on Saturday instead of Sunday, which was the day before Christmas. After church, Bruce made our Christmas dinner of his "killer" prime rib and twice-baked potatoes. The Woolleys came over, and between dinner and dessert, we attended Christmas Eve Services with them at their church. As we entered the foyer of the First Baptist Church waiting to go into the sanctuary, we all got a good laugh. The other door opened, and in walked a cute girl who said (with surprise in her voice) "Paul!" She was a classmate of his and obviously happy that he had come to her church.

We had a pretty low-key Christmas, opening our gifts in the morning as the Cheese Puff baked. We worked a puzzle (or tried—it was a humdinger) and played several games of table shuffleboard. That Saturday of the family party, Pastor Dennis came by with a brand new table shuffleboard game for the boys. Late that afternoon we headed for Hollister for Christmas dinner at Tony and Lili's house. Her

Mom, Sisters and three nieces had arrived from Mexico City earlier that day. They are wonderful people, and we had a really nice time celebrating with them. They all love and embrace Joseph and Paul.

A few days after Christmas, we drove up to Pioneer to visit Robb and Anna. They now had four children under four years of age in their home. Little J.J's adoption was now final, and they had his older half brother and his younger brother as foster children. They also were caring for an adorable little girl who had been abandoned. All four of the children really enjoyed the attention that Paul and Joseph gave them. Robb and Anna were doing a fantastic job with these children. Though our visit was short, we really enjoyed our time together.

Before we knew it, New Year's Day, 2007 had come. This was a bit of a difficult day for me, because Bruce was leaving with a team of people to go to Sri Lanka to work on a children's school/orphanage there. They would be heading for the airport on New Year's night. This was the first time that I felt left out. I would have really enjoyed going with him, but of course, my place was at home with the boys. My feelings were truly conflicted. However, the Lord gave me the peace I needed to stay behind. I had a lot to look forward to in the next two weeks. Not only was I helping to hostess a baby shower for Lili the first Saturday in January, but the event of the winter was happening that same evening.

Chapter 24 — Winter Wonderland Ball

Shortly before the Christmas break, I had seen a sign on campus about the Winter Formal. It was going to be held the first Saturday after school began in the new year. One evening at dinner, I happened to ask the boys if they had thought about attending. Paul was open to the idea, but Joseph didn't see himself asking any girl to go to a formal dance with him. Bruce, ever the salesman really talked up the idea, but he was never able to close the deal (much to his dismay).

A few days later, I went to pick up the boys after soccer practice. Joseph told me that he was going to the Winter Ball. Of course, I was delighted and surprised! I asked him what made him change his mind. It seems as though Devony and Leilani Victor, a really cute and talented young lady in the youth group, had decided that they would invite the boys to go with them. I sure had fun teasing Bruce about the fact that all his sales abilities had been upstaged by two cute girls. Duh!

The boys purchased their tickets, and I took them to the local florist to select wrist corsages for the girls. A few days before Bruce left for Sri Lanka, we took the boys to a nearby men's store to see about renting tuxedos. As it turned out, they were having a great sale on nice men's suits. We decided that it made a lot more sense to buy them each a new suit that they could use for future events. We matched them up with new shirts and ties. We headed to a store in the mall to find some dress shoes at a better price than at the men's store.

When Debra Leigh had come for breakfast before Christmas, she said to the boys, "I didn't know what to get you for Christmas, so I wonder if I could give you a dancing lesson." This would be perfect to prime them for the Winter Ball. The day after New Years, I pushed back the furniture in the living room, and we had a ballroom dancing floor. I had called both Devony and Leilani, and they showed up for the lesson, too. Ian, our next door neighbor, had been invited to the winter ball at Aptos High, so he wanted to learn to dance, also. Debra invited Kelly McGuckin, so it turned out to be three girls and three boys. What fun it was to see them pick up on the dance steps! She had them change partners at certain intervals, so they got used to dancing with more than one partner. By the end of the morning, Debra and I were doing the swing, too. What a groovy way to start a new year!

I got to be the chauffeur that evening of Jan. 6th. The boys looked so sharp! We picked up Devony, and of course, both of us moms had to take pictures. Leilani would meet us there, as her family had a gig up in San Jose that afternoon. She was also entertaining at the Ball, so they had to set up her keyboard. Since the affair was taking place at a country club in Hollister, we left a bit early so that Tony and Lili and her family could see the boys all dressed up. Dinner was being served at the Ball, so we didn't have to go to a restaurant. After dropping them off, I went back to Tony's house, ate dinner with them, and hung out until it was time to pick the four back up. I arrived a bit early, so I went inside the lobby to wait. Mr. Sharp encouraged me to go look in the ballroom to see how nice it looked. I kind of peeked around the corner, because I didn't want the boys to think I was spying on them. Pretty soon, I heard them announce the last dance, and I waited as the students started coming out. I can't even begin to describe the huge smiles on Joseph and Paul's faces as they came into view. The girls seemed to have had a nice time, too. After the boys walked the girls to their respective doors, we finally made it home a little after 1:30 am. I couldn't remember the last time I'd been up that late!

Deanna Smith, Devony's mom, had casually said to the boys when we picked up Devony, "You ought to wear your suits to church in the morning." They sort of snickered, and I didn't think they had taken her seriously. When it was time to leave for church, they came out of their room all dressed up, even with their ties on! Speaking of those ties, I was really concerned that I wouldn't be able to help them with that. Bless his heart, Bruce tied them before he left—very loosely, so all they had to do was slip them on and tighten them. They were the hit of the morning, making a real fashion statement.

Everyone complimented them on how handsome they looked. Needless to say, I was one proud mom!

Senior Citizen Soccer Mom
Chapter 22

The boys were so excited that it was officially Soccer Season at Monte Vista. Their coach, Matt Bryant, had been in touch with them since the summer before. Occasionally they played informal games and practiced every chance they got. Matt was really excited about the season starting, because several of the foreign students were playing this year. As he put it, "I have an Asian invasion and the African nation" to work with. Ultimately, Paul was chosen for the Varsity team, and Joseph for the Junior Varsity. I was chosen to do my part in helping at the snack bar and cheering the teams on.

In our area, Soccer is a winter sport. (Many of the players are on the football team, which occupies the fall). There were times that we sat out in the cold—all bundled up, and other times with an umbrella. It was a lot of fun watching their games, and I found myself wishing that I knew more about the rules of Soccer. Bruce and I asked the boys, many times about offside calls and free kicks. Their teams competed with some much larger schools, so they didn't win too often. It didn't matter to them. They sometimes lost by double digits, and both boys, especially Paul, would walk off that field with the biggest smiles on their faces! They truly love the game of soccer.

One really chilly late afternoon in January, I had driven down to Monterey with Corine and one of the men who worked in the boys dorm—Matt Hirota. (He wanted to photograph both of the teams). After the game, a young man approached me and introduced himself as a sports writer for the Santa Cruz Sentinel. He asked if he could have my permission to do an article on the boys. I told him that it was all right with me, but that he needed to ask the boys. They had had a few opportunities prior to this to share their story—one time for a radio program. They just hadn't felt comfortable about it, due mostly (I think) to their perceived lack of ease with the English language. We, of course, never pushed it, since we wanted them to be totally comfortable and to give them the respect of making their own decision. He introduced himself to both of the boys that day, and since he was a friend of Matt Bryant, they agreed. The next week, Isaiah Guzman and a photographer came to the house. He interviewed the boys and us, and took various pictures. He also met them at school one day for some more pictures. We were really surprised to see the January 21, 2007 edition of the Sunday Sentinel. There in full color on the front page was a picture of the boys, with a really nice article, as well as other snapshots they had taken. We received such a positive response—even from people that we really didn't know. I felt so proud of those two, that they were willing to share their painful past!

During one game toward the end of the season, we noticed Paul limping off the field. When we inquired, he shared that he had pulled his groin muscle. It was still quite sore the rest of the week. We took him to the doctor, who ordered physical therapy twice a week. Thankfully, he sat out only about one or two games. Unfortunately, he had wanted to go out for the track team in the spring, but was unable to.

Soccer season sped all too fast. I had actually enjoyed being a Senior Citizen Soccer Mom. More than anything, I was so pleased with Joseph and Paul's attitudes. They were always upbeat, even when faced with defeat repeatedly. Though they spent a lot of time after school practicing, they still maintained good grades. I must add, that we had a fairly dry and warm winter. The umbrellas didn't have to come out too much!

Warm Winter

Chapter 23

As the soccer season progressed, so did the boys, in all areas. After the first semester ended in January, they had report cards of mostly A's and B's. Monte Vista has a unique and wonderful week between semesters, called Jan-Term. A large variety of classes are offered, and many people from the community come in to teach. There are classes from dirt bike riding, quilt making, calligraphy, cake decorating, working at an animal shelter or a food kitchen—to name a few. Several overseas missions trips are also offered. Our boys ended up taking a hiking class. Each day they would explore an area of our county such as the Elkhorn Slough Nature Trail, the Redwoods, etc. They thoroughly enjoyed it along with the nice water bottles they were given by the hiking expert, Mr. B. He also provided nice snacks for them. It never rained on them the entire week.

In early February, we had a special visitor for a long weekend. It was our African American friend from Baton Rouge, Tarrin James. Bruce had met him at a conference at the Bethany World Pray

Center some years ago. They took a liking to each other from the get-go. Tarrin had invited Bruce and Pastor Dennis to his home for a cell group meeting. Shortly thereafter, Tarrin brought his wife, Denise, out to visit us, and we have maintained a friendship. He has also brought some of his buddies out through the years. This man is so full of the joy of the Lord, that our home feels anointed when he is around. We hadn't seen him for quite awhile, and he really wanted to meet Joseph and Paul. What a great time we had during his visit, and it was so wonderful to see the boys laughing with him and enjoying his Southern accent!

That same weekend, we had received an invitation to Mayra Flores' 18th birthday. It was to be held at the beach. However, that Saturday was cold and overcast. Bruce called Mills and offered to host the party at our house. Sure enough, it started to rain late that afternoon. That didn't dampen our spirits at all, as the party was relocated. Many of the people that came had met Tarrin during his prior visits, so he thoroughly enjoyed himself. Of course, Paul and Joseph had a great time, too.

On the Monday evening after Tarrin departed, I got a call to substitute teach the next day. I told Laura (the gal that lines up the subs) that we had a grandbaby that was due the next day—Feb. 20th. "But, how many babies (especially first-borns) actually arrive on their due dates? "I'll be there," I told her. I reported to school the next day, and made it through the first period. I had told Bruce that I'd keep my cell phone on (something that I don't normally do when subbing), just in case. Sure enough, second period came around, and I received a call from Bruce. Lili was going to the doctor and there was a good chance that she'd head to the hospital from his office. Stay tuned. Cell phone reception at the school is sketchy at best. By third period, I received a call from the office. Bruce hadn't been able to get through, so he left the message that she was definitely headed to the hospital. There was a good chance that TJ (Tony Junior) was going to be born that day. I was excited to say the least! Thankfully Steve Miles, the vice principal, showed up to take over the class until they could get a "sub" for the "sub". Lili had invited me to be in the delivery room, and this would be a first. When the other grandchildren were born, we never made it in time. We had a three-hour drive, and the babies came fast. I headed up to San Jose and found the hospital. Lili was definitely in the midst of labor. She was so strong! About three hours after my arrival, our precious grandson faced the world. What a blessed gift it was to watch God's miracle unfold! Bruce and I were so thrilled!

Mama and baby came home from the hospital that Thursday afternoon. I prepared a meal to take over to their home. Her mother and sister had spent time with her during the hospital stay, so I wanted to bless them all. The boys helped me load the food into the car, and off we went. I will forever cherish the memory of Paul and Joseph each holding this newborn with those huge grins on their faces!

President's holiday weekend came around, and

Craig brought Amber, Dominic and Kaitlin to stay for a couple of days. Of course, we played lots of UNO and worked their favorite puzzles. The weather was so warm that we enjoyed time at the beach. As usual, Paul and Joseph had a good time with their nieces and nephew. Of course, GramS and GrandpaB did, too!

Unfortunately, we didn't get much skiing in this particular winter. In early March, though, we found our way up to Tahoe with the Miracles, again. Paul was still nursing his pulled hamstring muscle, so he hung out with Sephy at the condo and got some homework done. Bruce, Joseph, and I had a good day of skiing, and we were both impressed with how Joseph picked it right up again. He skied along with us, and kept going by himself when we got tuckered out. Of course, that big grin of his made it fun for us.

After soccer season was over, one of the teachers at Monte Vista—Josh Davis—decided to put together a boy's volleyball team. This wasn't a sanctioned sport at the school, but there were students who wanted to play. Joseph signed up for the team and really enjoyed learning a new American sport. He also met some students that he hadn't known before. They practiced a couple of days a week after school and played a few games. Once, they went up to San Jose to play a school there. We were proud of him for taking advantage of an opportunity to stretch himself.

Easter in Montana

Chapter 24

Throughout the winter, we were thinking about a trip to Montana to visit my sister, Kitty, for Easter. All the arrangements were made, and very early on Good Friday morning we were on our way to the airport to fly to Spokane. There, we picked up a rental car and drove the three hours to Polson, Montana. This was the first time we had all flown together, and a first for the boys since their lengthy flights to America.

We arrived to a beautiful, sunny, clear morning in Eastern Washington. The ride across the mountains from Spokane was packed with beautiful scenery, though there was some snoozing going on in the back seat (due to such an early departure).

What a wonderful time we had! My nephew, David Vaughan and his wife, Amy, along with Amy's parents bought an 80 acre farm near Ronan, Mt. On our drive from Missoula toward Polson, we stopped by, since it was on our way. They have a lovely place with views of the snow-capped mountains. It was so good to see him, and he looked so happy with his farm.

We were surprised to see Flathead Lake when we drove into Polson. It is huge, and we had a view of it from Kitty's home. It was wonderful to see her, since it had been a year and a half. She had not met Paul yet. We had a nice dinner across the street at our motel (which was on the lake), and spent the evening playing Skipbo.

Saturday dawned warm and sunny. After baking a bunny cake for the next day and having breakfast at Kitty's place, we set out to do some sightseeing. We drove to the National Bison Range where we got some great pictures of buffalo and elk. Of great interest to all of us was the tall pile of antlers that stood higher than the boys. We also visited the nearby St. Ignatius Mission that was built in 1891.

We were up early on Easter to go to the first service at my sister's church. They served a wonderful breakfast afterward, and we got to meet several of her friends. We also attended the second service in celebration of our Lord's Resurrection.

That afternoon, we headed back out to David's farm. The weather was warm and sunny—a picture perfect day, with the mountains glistening in the distance. My great niece, Hannah, came running to greet us, but her younger brother, Phillip, held back. David and Amy saddled up two of their riding horses, and the boys got to ride. They certainly enjoyed their first ride on a horse! Soon, Phillip warmed up to the boys, and they played lots of catch with him. He was upset when it was time for Paul and Joseph to leave.

We ended up the afternoon at Amy's parents'

new home at the far corner of the farm. Michal and Frank had prepared a wonderful Easter meal for us all. It was such a pleasant day, and all around us was the grandeur of God's glorious creation and the rebirth of the grasses and wildflowers. It was truly a day to rejoice in the Resurrection!

On Monday morning, we had planned a trip to Glacier National Park with Kitty. However, it was pouring rain. What a difference a day makes! As we drove up the mountain, visibility was not good, so we decided to wait until a return visit to see Glacier. Instead, we drove to Kalispell, had lunch, and drove the other way around Flathead Lake to Polson.

We said good-bye to Kitty and drove to Sandpoint, Idaho to stay for a few days. We had never spent any time in this part of the West, and we wanted to explore new vistas. Then we went on to Coeur D'Alene, Idaho and back to Spokane. In our few days there, we enjoyed Riverfront Park, Cat's Paws (a zoo that rescues endangered animals), and the Museum of Art and Culture (MAC) that had a special exhibit called Sudan: The Land and the People. The boys really enjoyed that, and we learned a lot about their country from the wonderful display of pictures. It was a nice, relaxing time for us as a family. Paul was really enjoying our many games of Skipbo. We even played at the airport while waiting for our plane. He just couldn't seem to lose—much to my chagrin!

Showers of Blessings

Chapter 25

After returning from Easter break, the school year was moving rapidly. The boys were to take the TOEFFL test—an English language proficiency test, that we heard was quite difficult. We had heard that in order to stay at Monte Vista, they had to pass this test. We tried some on-line practices, which proved to be rather hard for them. Thankfully, a wonderful lady at our church who teaches ESL classes at Cabrillo College, stepped up to offer her services as a tutor to the students in ESL. Linda Buie really liked the boys, and she helped them prepare.

The evening of test day, we received a call from Mr. McCroskey. He wanted to break the news that neither of the boys had made the required score. (Several other foreign students had not, either.) I asked Joe what he would advise me to do. He suggested that we call the Foreign Student Enrollment Advisor, Pete Gieseke, so that we could figure something out for the boys' future.

First thing the next morning, I was on the phone with Mr. Gieseke, and we arranged for an appointment at 9:30 am. Of course, Bruce and I were in prayer. As we arrived, Pete was looking over their test results. He looked up at us and said, "Wow, these boys have sure made good progress this year!" Needless to say, we both breathed a sigh of relief. The rest of the meeting was to determine a course for them for the next year. It was decided that we would take advantage of the Resource Classes in English and Math for the boys. Linda Mulliner, who was the current registrar, sat in with us. Both of them agreed that Monte Vista really was pleased with Joseph and Paul, and that they would work with us to make a plan for the remainder of their high school education. We were so grateful that our prayers had been answered by our Heavenly Father, and that Monte Vista cared so much for these boys!

Little did we know how much they really cared. A few weeks later, I received a phone call from an MV student. He wanted to let us know that there would be a Character Awards Assembly the next week at the school. He informed me that Joseph and Paul would be receiving an award, and invited us to attend. We were not to tell them, because it was a surprise.

There was great excitement in the gym the following Tuesday morning when we arrived. One of the senior girls met us as we stepped inside and showed us to the chairs up at the front of the gym where the parents were seated. We learned that each year teachers nominate about five students from each grade that match certain Biblical characters. Then the students vote for the top two that exemplify that quality. Both Paul and Joseph were awarded the Paul Award "to a student who has overcome a special hardship or adversity." On the beautifully framed awards is the scripture from I Peter 2:20: "But if you suffer for doing good and you endure it, this is commendable before God." All the recipients of each of the character awards received a wonderful applause. However, as Joseph and Paul went forward (individually), the audience burst forth with a gigantic applause that continued for some time. Bruce and I were—of course—overwhelmed by such an amazing affirmation for our boys. I found myself in tears—off and on—that entire day! On the way home I said to Bruce, "Honey, imagine the blessings that we would have missed if we hadn't listened to the Lord's prompting to receive Joseph and Paul." I was truly humbled, to think that we had come close to missing such a blessing. Later that day, on our answering machine was a message from Linda Buie (whose daughter, Serena, had also received a character award) stating how wonderful it was that the school had honored Paul and Joseph in such a spectacular way.

Late in May, we were blessed, yet again, when the boys brought home their school yearbook. The title on the front of the book is "Momentous 2007." The book opens with the definition of Momentous (adj.)—of utmost importance; of outstanding significance or consequence. The first few pages feature students in such as "A Moment of Service," "A Moment of Transformation," (which, incidentally, featured the boys' friend—Jason—from China who accepted Christ), "A Moment of Clarity," "A Moment of Truth," and "A Moment of Hope". There in the section entitled "A Moment of Hope" was a full-page colored picture of Joseph and Paul. The adjacent page had a few more pictures of them along with the following:

"On a day like any other, cousins Paul Yana and Joseph Kelly, were tending to cattle when their lives changed forever. Screams of terror broke out as Muslim militia overran their village without mercy. Gunshots rang out as screams echoed through the village. Paul and Joseph had been taught to run and not to return home at the sound of gunfire. "We just ran, and we didn't look back," explains Joseph. They did as they were told and ran from their home and all that they had ever known. They were not alone during the beginning of their journey. They traveled with a group of boys of similar age. Together, under the cloak of the night, they crept from village to village in hope of refuge. Time and time again they were turned away, seen as nothing more than mouths to feed. The boys continued to travel, and survived off of pond water and whatever fruit they could find. Slowly, the group began to shrink. Unfortunate endings came upon some of the other boys in their party. In three separate crossings of the Nile River some of Joseph and Paul's friends were attacked by crocodiles, and others were attacked by lions in the African plains. Eventually they found haven in a United Nations' Sherkole Refugee Camp in Ethiopia. It was there that Joseph and Paul spent the next five years of their lives. In this camp they lived in a grass hut and were given fifteen kilograms of grain and cooking oil every month. The camp not only gave the boys a place to eat and sleep, but also served as a place of learning. Together, the boys took classes such as math and Bible. The refugee camp is where the pair learned English, and for the first time heard of the United States. Through the Catholic Charities Organization, Joseph was allowed to come to the United States in September, 2005. Paul joined him two months later, both having what was equivalent to a fifth-grade education. Though to escape such terror seems to be a pure blessing, it was not an easy adjustment. American food was not familiar, and washing machines and dishwashers seemed funny to them. Neither of the boys had taken a shower before relocating to the States. Escaping Sudanese civil war, the cousins take residence on a vegetable and strawberry farm with loving foster parents, Mr. and Mrs. Bruscia, but they have no knowledge of whether or not their own families are still alive. "Sometimes I dream I meet with my brothers . . . then I wake up," says Paul of his family. They hope one day to return to their homeland and find out."

Summer of '07
Chapter 26

The boys had worked hard since the last summer and were making great strides on their English. We had prayed and thought about the upcoming summer. They really needed a break from school, so we didn't seriously consider summer school. There was the possibility of jobs, though they continued to work on Saturdays for Bruce when they could, and he paid them better than a fast-food job. They also worked as time permitted for Doug, a neighbor, who has a business of screen-printing on shirts, jackets, etc. We realized that this might be our last chance to do something special with the boys, since school and jobs would be a necessity in the future. We knew how much it would mean to them to be able to reunite with their friends back East. The boys helped us to decide on a three-week trip to the East Coast to combine a visit with their friends, along with some hands-on U.S. History. We also decided to invite our granddaughter, Amber, along. She would be entering 8th Grade in the fall, and we felt that this would be a good opportunity for her to get in on the history, too. Besides, she gets along famously with

Joseph and Paul. They have a lot of fun together.

Plans were made, and a few days after school was out—June 12th, the five of us flew to Baltimore. There was a delay in Las Vegas, so we arrived really late or should I say, early in the morning. By the time we waited in line to get our rental car and made our way to the hotel we had reserved, it was way past 3:00 am. They hadn't placed a roll-away bed in the room, as we had requested. Bruce and the boys had to carry one up a flight of stairs (no elevator) so Amber would have a place to sleep. They were learning all about flexibility in travel. We all slept very late the next morning, except Bruce. When I awoke at about 11:00 a.m. (the latest I had slept in ages), I noticed that Bruce had crept out of the room. The kids were still asleep. I went into the bathroom and thought I'd get my shower out of the way. I tried to turn it on, but nothing came out. Given my lack of mechanical ability, I thought at first, that I just didn't know how to work it. I went to turn on the sink, and alas, no water! About that time, Bruce returned. He had in his hand a notice placed on our door that morning which stated there would be no water from about 10:00a.m. until 2:00 p.m. that day, due to repairs. (They had never mentioned this when we checked in earlier that morning.) They brought up a couple of buckets of water so that we could flush the toilet. As Bruce was calling the agency that had booked us at this place, the kids and I got on our bathing suits—we could swim instead of shower. Great idea, huh? Well, we finally found the pool (which was not an easy fete in this place), only to discover that it wasn't opened. Needless to say, we packed up, as by this time, the hotel service had booked us at another, much nicer place. This was quite the start of our adventures!

After stopping off for lunch, we headed into the Baltimore Harbor. There is a wonderful tourist center there to assist in plans for seeing the city. Our first stop was to the Top of the World. This has an awesome view of Baltimore and the harbor, as well as exhibits that helped us learn more about the city. After coming back down, we took a fascinating tour of the USS Constellation. The boys found it very interesting that the first tour of duty this ship was ordered to make was for slave boat interdiction off the coast of Africa. By then, it was getting pretty late, and the sky was threateningly dark. Just after Bruce, Joseph and Amber got into the parking garage, the skies opened up. Paul and I were somewhat undercover at a bus-stop where they would pick us up. I was still nursing a pulled hamstring muscle from a fall. I was also healing from a broken bone on top of my left foot. I wasn't up to walking the several blocks to the car. It poured cats and dogs, as I explained to Paul who laughed when he realized what I meant. He was quite enthralled since we hadn't seen buckets of rain like that in such a short time since he had been here.

The next few days, we enjoyed more sights of Baltimore. It seemed particularly fitting that on Flag Day, we took the water taxi over to Ft. McHenry. We all thoroughly enjoyed learning about the history of our national anthem. At the end of the introductory film, the Star Spangled Banner is sung. The curtain opens up on a large window displaying a huge American flag blowing in the breeze. I had a tear in my eye and goosebumps. I thanked the Lord—once again—that I had been born in this great, free country! How grateful I felt that I could share this freedom with these special young men who hadn't—as yet—experienced, but a small taste of it.

At the Baltimore Science Museum, they just happened to have "The Wonder of the Nile" playing at the IMAX theater. It was so interesting and well done; and it gave us a clearer picture of how difficult it must have been for the boys to swim across it to safety!

Our last stop in Baltimore was a morning at the wonderful Aquarium. I know the three kids enjoyed it, but the boys were getting a bit antsy. Afterward we were leaving for Philadelphia. They were so excited to see their friends! When they parted company back in Ethiopia, they never dreamed that they would see them again. We drove through Amish country on the way. The horse buggies, dark clothing and caps were certainly of interest to the three in the back seat. We stopped at the Bird-in-Hand Farmer's Market and enjoyed sampling some of the local foods and crafts.

We found our motel, settled in, and Bruce drove the boys a short way north to Souderton. Their life-long friends eagerly awaited their arrival. According to Bruce, it was quit the reunion—smiles, hugs, jumping up and down! The boys grasped each other in a small circle of love and jumped for joy for several minutes. He had tears in his eyes just telling me about it. He brought a carload of the boys back to our motel to swim and eat pizza that we had ordered. These wonderful young men were all smiles, and every bit as sweet and genuine as Joseph and Paul. They spent the evening reminiscing and talking about their new life. I felt so privileged to meet them all, and they seemed happy to meet Joseph and Paul's "white mama."

Their friends had to work the next day, so we went to see the Liberty Bell and toured around Philadelphia on a double decker bus. We got a good feel for the "local flavor." Afterward, the boys got to visit their friends that evening, too.

The next day we stopped at the Betsy Ross House and toured the African American Museum. After enjoying a Philly Cheesesteak Sandwich, we kept our appointment for a tour of Carpenter Hall. It got pretty warm that afternoon, so we headed back to the hotel to swim. The friends joined us that evening for a picnic by the pool, and to play some basketball and swim. It was a difficult good-bye, but all the boys said they would accept our invitation to come to California to visit us. I was really touched, as one of the boys gave Paul the bright red basketball shoes that he was wearing (and that Paul was admiring!)

After our wonderful stay in Philadelphia, we drove on to New York City. Our first stop there (the next morning), was to visit the Statue of Liberty. An amazing thing happened! As we were making our way through the long line of people, we saw some friends of ours—actually, neighbors (we can see their home on the next hill across the road from ours)— Steve and Anne Nelson and their two daughters, Jessica and Emily. We hadn't connected with them for awhile, so it was fun riding the boat over and catching up. We five got off at Ellis Island first, and then the Statue of Liberty. Later, we were able to see ground zero and Central Park. A stop at the Carnegie Deli for one of their pastrami sandwiches was a must. The three really enjoyed the double-decker bus tour of New York City at night. They were captivated by all the lights, as well as all the people out and about. Joseph and Paul said that New York City reminded them of their fun stay in San Francisco. What a huge contrast to our quiet farm. Incidentally, it was a bit humorous that I found myself in New York (a place I'm not particularly fond of) on my 31st anniversary—with three youngsters in our room!

We were back to our hotel room rather late that evening, so we relaxed quite a bit the next day. We were staying in Queens, so we drove out to Coney Island. We had never been there, so we all enjoyed seeing it and having a "Coney Island" hot dog. It was the first time that Joseph, Paul, and Amber got to put their feet into the Atlantic Ocean.

Our next jaunt was on to Massachusetts. We first took a short drive to Concord and visited Minuteman National Park. We had never heard of this place, but found it to be fascinating! We watched the well-done film about the beginning of the Revolutionary

War and were directed to a place in the park where a man would be firing a rifle like the ones they used back then. It was really interesting to learn about the weapons, and we all plugged our ears, as he took a few shots with it. The boys found this demonstration quite interesting.

After checking in, we headed into Worcester to find some more of the boys' friends. This time, I got to see the reunion first hand, and it was truly a joyous occasion! Again, so much love, joy, and emotion was on display. We all walked several blocks to a pizza parlor where the boys were able to visit. We spent the next day on the Old Town Trolley in Boston, getting off at certain places we wanted to see—the Boston Common, Faneil Marketplace, etc. The tour bus driver was particularly interested in the boys and asked them a lot of questions.

Their friends were occupied the next day, so we drove out to Cape Cod where we enjoyed the Flea Market and the Heritage Museum in Sandwich. The boys negotiated several purchases on their own. We ended the day in Plymouth, so they could see Plymouth Rock (or Plymouth Pebble, as we fondly call it, since it is quite eroded), We enjoyed a nice seafood dinner there. The next day, we had a fantastic time at Old Sturbridge Village until their friends were free. Afterward, the boys got to go play soccer with them in the park and visit one last time. Again, the good-bye was difficult at best. It was heartwarming, never-the-less, to see some of the 50 survivors reunited with such joy.

We decided that we wanted to spend a bit more

time in Amish Country on our way to Washington D.C. We drove to Lancaster County, PA to spend the afternoon and evening. The kids seemed quite interested in the Amish way of life, so we all went to see a movie "Jacob's Choice" (very well done) and toured an Amish home. We found a nice Amish smorgasbord that evening and enjoyed looking at the Amish Craft stores in the area.

Our last leg of the journey was to D.C. Our wonderfully pleasant weather had disappeared, and it had turned really hot and muggy! The boys were experiencing what an Eastern summer could be like. As we checked into our hotel in Arlington, Joseph commented, "I miss my own bed." This was a significant comment to us, because it provided us with an answer to a question before we came on the trip. We had discussed the possibility that Joseph and Paul might express some hesitation about returning to our home after spending time in an area with so many of their friends. It was heartwarming to see that Joseph was reflecting positively on his new American home.

We took a tour of the Capitol our first day. While Amber and I went to the Arboretum across the street, Bruce took the boys to meet Sam Farr, our U.S. Representative. He expressed a true interest in the boys and their life, and asked them several questions. Congressman Farr spent quite a bit of time with the boys before introducing them to a lady on his staff who is in charge of African affairs. They discussed with her—first hand— the struggles that continue in Sudan. After lunch at Union Station, we took the subway back to Pentagon City and enjoyed cooling off in the pool.

The next morning, we got on the subway again (the kids really got a kick out of riding it) to visit some of the Smithsonians. The Space Museum was wonderful, and we especially enjoyed NASA's IMAX theatre presentation of the Space Station. After a stroll through the African Art Museum, we were heading back to the subway when the sky opened up and we were poured on. It came down really fast and left every bit as rapidly. We were soaked by the time we got to the subway, and it helped to cool us off.

There is so much to do and see in D.C., so we asked them to choose some of the attractions they were interested in. Paul really wanted to see an elephant, so we all headed the next day to the National Zoo. This is a fantastic attraction! He had a huge smile, as I snapped a picture of him and the elephant. I think it helped him to feel a connection back to his roots in Africa.

The next morning, we were all excited about the visit that day with my niece, Susie Jo and Don who were on their way to North Carolina. We had arranged our D.C. stay at the end of our travels to co-ordinate with their trip. We all went on the D.C. Duck Tour. By now, it had cooled down and was really pleasant. Later that evening, we were able to see the Washington and Lincoln monuments and the Korean and World War II Memorials. Honest Abe looked great with the lights shining on him!

Susie and D had to head out by the next afternoon.

Their last morning, we all took a tour of Arlington National Cemetery and the Arlington House before we had to say our good-byes.

Our trip was about to end, but we still squeezed in a fabulous free concert of patriotic music at the Kennedy Center and a ride out to Monticello. (We had visited Mr. Vernon a few times prior, but had never been able to get a reservation to see Thomas Jefferson's place). Though it was a wonderful trip, the three kids were on information overload; and we were all looking forward to getting back home. We arrived in San Jose late on the 4th of July and were met by Tony, Lili and T.J. We were able to see fireworks from the car on the way home.

The next morning, Tony got up early to participate in a golf tournament. I was sure the boys were still asleep in their own beds. I looked out the kitchen window, and much to my surprise, they were both walking around outside talking to each other in Mabaan. They seemed truly happy to be back on the farm!

Our time at home, however, was short-lived. The following Sunday after church, we left for Chico to attend Donnie Moore Radical Reality Camp. Bruce and I had been asked to be part of the program team, and we drove up there with some of the other leadership. The boys rode up on the bus with all the other campers from our church.

Usually, it is really hot up in Chico in the summer, but the Lord was so good to us this year! It was unusually cool, and we even experienced a little bit of rain, which is highly unusual in the middle of summer. Our cabin was rather rustic, but with the help of a blow-up mattress we had thrown in at the last minute, we were able to get some sleep—me on the old, saggy double bed and Bruce on the mattress.

It turned out to be a super experience for the boys. In their respective cabins, they were able to really bond with some of the guys in the youth group. They seemed to enjoy the activities, and Bruce and I were so thrilled to see them at the altar praying each night. Their first exposure to Youth Camp had, indeed, been a success. "Grandpa and Grandma" Counselors came home pretty tired, yet invigorated and spiritually full from all of the wonderful messages that had been presented. Donnie Moore spoke, as did Tim Dilena (from the Revival Tabernacle in Highland Park, near Detroit where we had served on two previous missions trips). Joey Steelman, a member of Donnie's team gave a great message, too. Of course, we were totally encouraged by the response of our youth, and their renewed dedication to serving our Lord!

After Radical Reality Camp, we had a week off, and then our church's Kid's Summer Adventure (Vacation Bible School) was to take place. I had talked to Joseph and Paul about being helpers. I was in charge of "Chatter's Theater"—one of the four stations that the children came to each day. I kept encouraging them by reminding them how good they were with children. Also, they could earn all of their community service hours for the upcoming school year. I couldn't quite convince them. The best I could do was to talk them into going with me to the meeting the Wednesday evening before the event was to begin. Well, what I couldn't talk them into, Pastor Peter Bobbitt could! By the end of the evening, they—along with Shane Titus (who had to work a few of the days)—were going to be the leaders of a group of boys. During the next few days we were preparing my room as well as setting up a station for them.

What a great job Joseph and Paul did! The young boys really liked them, and they had giant smiles on their faces all week. In fact, Belinda Bell, one of the directors of Kids Summer Adventure made the comment that Joseph and Paul were her "afternoon coffee." When she felt like she needed a pick-me-up, she would just look at their smiles and become re-invigorated. Kids Summer Adventure was a huge success, and Joseph and Paul earned all their community service hours.

We now had a few weeks at home, and boy, were we working on the summer reading project that was assigned by Monte Vista! Since we had played so much thus far, it was now necessary to hit it hard. The book for sophomores was *Cry the Beloved Country*, which is actually three books in one. We worked several hours each day, knowing that a written paper would need to be completed by the first day of school.

The first week of August, we took a break from the reading. The boys were headed up to Santa Clara University for their second experience at Soccer Camp. This time, they packed an air-conditioner (Joseph's name for a room fan), as well as a big container of deodorizing powder for their stinky soccer shoes! As with Radical Reality Camp, the weather was much kinder to them than it had been the year before. They thoroughly enjoyed it once again. Bruce and I headed for the airport the day that they started camp. We were going to have a few days to ourselves up in Spokane. My sister, Margaret (aka, Kitty) from Montana and her grandchildren, as well as their other grandmother, Michal, joined us for a beautiful day at Riverfront Park. It was a really enjoyable and relaxing time. Our plane landed back in San Jose that Friday in time for us to pick the boys up from Soccer Camp. Of course, they were sporting those wonderful smiles and had had a great time!

By now, there was but one week left before school—which started early this year—August 20th. Though none of us felt quite ready for this wonderful summer to end, we had to face reality. Much effort was put into finishing the summer homework. Of course, we spent some time cleaning their room—drawers and closets—and getting organized for school.

Sophomore Year
Chapter 27

After what seemed to be a fast summer break, both boys were happy to be back at Monte Vista, where they felt loved and accepted. One day, as we were in the car returning from Kids Summer Adventure, Joseph said, "Sue, I'd like to play football this year." It took me a few seconds to gain my composure. (You see, when he first arrived and had seen his first American NFL game on TV, he couldn't believe how different it was from what he knew as football, namely Soccer. He once said "I wouldn't want to play that and get knocked down!)"

I replied, "Well, let's talk to Bruce about it when we get home."

Bruce shared with him how physical a game it was, and that injuries often occur. However, if he really wanted to try, we wouldn't stand in his way. That afternoon, they went to school to speak to the coach. Practice had already started (though school had not yet begun), and the coach explained that any boy who wanted to play—as long as their grades were maintained—could play. We paid the fee, and Joseph began practicing and learning about American football. Since Bruce had played and coached football, he would throw passes at Joseph and give him lots of pointers.

Over Labor Day Weekend, Joseph traveled with the teams—he was on the Junior Varsity team—to San Diego to play a game and visit some colleges there. He was learning a lot and enjoying the camaraderie of being on a team. We were proud of him for "stepping out" and trying something brand new.

This second year proved to be really challenging for us. No longer in ESL (only one year is provided at the school), they would now be in regular classes. This meant competing with students who had been in school for 10 years and used English all of their lives. Due to missing out on some of the Freshman requirements because of ESL classes, the boys found themselves behind the normal 4 year path to graduation. They would be taking Earth Science, as well as Health Science, Algebra 1 B (the second half of Algebra), and Resource English (a smaller class with more help). Paul had U.S. History and Beginning Choir/Bible. Joseph had Advanced Photography and Bible. We were happy to be able to enroll Joseph and Paul into a Resource Class with tutorial help. The new Resource teachers, Sue Verutti and Jackie Goble, expressed how much they enjoyed helping Joseph and Paul.

From day one, the homework started—and lots of it! Obviously, the boys needed a lot of help. So, usually nights at our home consisted of Bruce helping one and me the other—or taking turns if they were working on the same subject. Thankfully, Karen was still tutoring them in Math. So many of the concepts in Health, Science, and Social Studies are totally foreign to them. It took a lot of explaining and re-explaining. I must admit, at times I was really overwhelmed with the enormity of the task! Many nights, I was tired, and homework was the last thing I wanted to do. I had to ask the Lord—often—to give me strength. He always comes through! I must admit that my attitude toward homework wasn't the best. (I never much liked it when I was in school—or when our first set of children had to do it, either.) I prayed about my attitude, and God is faithful. He has helped me see it as a challenge and a chance to re-learn many interesting things. It has become more bearable, but I jokingly tell my friends—"three times and I'm out!"

The teachers have, for the most part, been very helpful and cooperative with us. The personnel at Monte Vista, I believe, really want to see the boys succeed. I sense that—at times—the boys get discouraged, so we are constantly encouraging them. We keep saying, "We believe in you and what our Lord can accomplish through you." It sure takes hard work! I'm happy to say that they are making it, and they both had good enough grades to play soccer.

Autumn sure went fast. We enjoyed our renewed interest in football games. Joseph didn't get to play very much (way less chance of getting hurt), but he kept a great attitude through all of his practices. He learned a lot about American football, too. Because of his new-found knowledge, both boys have found football more interesting and often join us in watching NFL games on TV

As the first semester came to a close, the boys were working more and more on their own. Though it is still a struggle, they both really liked being at Monte Vista. Due to the fact that school had begun so early, the first semester was finished (and final exams completed) by the time Christmas vacation came around. It was a much-needed break that we all looked forward to!

It was especially exciting, since their friend they had seen in Philadelphia, Musa, was flying out to join us for Christmas. He had some difficulty with his travel arrangements, due to a big storm back East. He finally arrived—three days after we had originally expected him. Bruce had been in touch with the airlines and with Musa to reschedule him. We got a chuckle out of the phone call that Paul received when Musa was at the airport in Philadelphia finally ready to board the plane. He called Paul in a panic because "they took my suitcase and wouldn't give it back to me!" Thankfully, since Paul had traveled domestically with us, he was able to explain to Musa that his bag would be waiting for him when he arrived in San Jose!

We had lots of fun things planned for our special guest—a jaunt up to San Francisco, ice skating with the other URM kids, a trip to the Monterey Bay Aquarium, and generally showing him around our area. He enjoyed the mild, sunny days and the late nights of playing dominos. Most of all, Paul and

Joseph seemed to gain a lot of joy in introducing Musa to their new world.

The day after New Years, we took Musa to the airport and hopped on a plane ourselves to go back to Spokane. We wanted to look at some properties and do a little skiing. We asked the boys if they might want to learn to snowboard instead of ski this time. They both thought that sounded like a good idea, so we signed them up for a lesson. They really enjoyed it! In fact, we couldn't get Joseph off of the practice hill after the lesson was over, to eat his lunch. Finally, when he took a break, he informed us that he was no longer a skier. "Snowboarding rules," he explained. Teasingly, he added as he looked at Bruce, "Skiing is for old men."

The special Jan-term classes were held right after Christmas break, which was a great way to get back into the swing of things. Paul took bowling in the mornings and circus stunts in the afternoon. He learned how to juggle, do flips and ride on a unicycle. (The latter activity, he felt, was more suited to girls!) Joseph took an adventures class. Each day they did something different. Day one was a hike in the Santa Cruz mountains. Day two was laser tag (which he really enjoyed). Day three was a whale watching trip in the Monterey Bay, in which all but about three of the students got sea sick—Joseph included. Day four, they took a bicycle ride, and the last day was a trip to play paintball. They both enjoyed Jan-term, and we were happy that they were able to experience new activities.

Following Jan-term, soccer season was in full

swing. Both boys played on the Varsity team, and the team won several games this year. Paul actually made about eight goals throughout the season— one of which was on my birthday. There was an extra fan there that day, as my niece, Susie Jo had flown in to surprise me with a visit. Of course, those huge smiles were on both of their faces as they walked off the field.

The Winter Ball came, again, in January. This year, both boys invited a date to go with them. Both ended up attending with cute young ladies who were Seniors. Susie Jo was still visiting on the evening of the ball. She really enjoyed seeing Joseph and Paul all dressed up with their dates. She stood between these handsome young men for a picture, too. Since neither of the boys could drive yet, Bruce was feeling that it would be a huge embarrassment to them to have their dad drive them. So, ever the creative one, he contacted our friend, Jordan Stidham. He was about to finish his undergrad degree at California State University— Monterey Bay. He works with the youth at church, and is a super young man. Bruce hired him to drive the boys and their dates in our van. While the four were at the Winter Ball, he and his girlfriend had dinner out and attended a movie. They then picked up the kids at the dance and all stopped for a bite to eat before arriving back home—sometime in the wee hours of the morning. We didn't even hear them come in! We could see that they were gaining a great deal of confidence in the area of dating in this American culture.

Midway through the school year, we had to make a decision about their schooling for the following year. At this point, the government had Joseph at 19 years old, and he still had two years left of high school. He mentioned to us that he was feeling too old to be in high school. After much prayer and consideration, Bruce took both of the boys out to Cabrillo College—a local junior college located in Aptos. They talked to a person in the admissions office, who arranged for them to come back for a tour of the campus. Joseph decided that he would like to attend there. We were proud of him for being secure enough to step out of the safe environment that he had become accustomed to. Paul wanted to go back to Monte Vista for his junior year, and plans to continue there until graduation. We felt that a separation would be good for them, as they could develop more of their individual identity. We had much peace about the decision. The remainder of their sophomore year sped by.

In May, they had another opportunity to stretch themselves. A year and a half prior, a professor at the University of California—Santa Cruz, Dr. Tony Hoffman, had seen the article in the Santa Cruz Sentinel about the boys. He got our phone number (with our permission) from the writer, and contacted us. He teaches a class on "Children of War" and wanted to see if Joseph and Paul would come and talk to his class. At that time, they were still too self-conscious about their English skills and didn't want to do that. Professor Hoffman stayed in touch with us, and a year later, the boys consented to go. It was agreed that a question-and-answer presentation would be the most comfortable for them. They were picked up at the house by Dr. Hoffman that morning, and had a wonderful time. He had arranged for cute young ladies to give them a tour of the campus. He took them to lunch at the Staff cafeteria, where they were introduced to the Chancellor. He also gave them a gift card for the student bookstore. It turned out to be a great experience for them! A few weeks later, a large envelope arrived in the mail for the boys. It was a stack of "thank you letters" from the students in the class, who had many encouraging remarks for Joseph and Paul.

Here are some of those remarks. One student said, "It undoubtedly took a lot of courage to stand up in front of a lot of strangers. It reflected strongly upon your character as outstanding young men." Another wrote, "In the whole hour that you were here, I learned more than in the years I have been in the university." Yet, another student commented, "The two of you are extremely strong and powerful individuals. Your experiences will stay with me for the rest of my life." Another wrote, "I was amazed by your story and what you had to say about moving here. I can't imagine the amount of courage you must have to be able to go through what you did, and come to America without knowing anyone here." Finally, "I wanted to thank you for coming in and talking to the class. I really appreciate being able to hear your story. A lot of times I can get so sheltered and so desensitized by the barrage of images on TV that I forget about the actual people in these situations. Hearing the story from your own lips truly moved me." It even turned out that one of the girls in the class contacted Joseph, and they met at the Boardwalk one afternoon in early June before she returned to her home in San Diego for the summer. They have continued to stay in touch.

One of the first accomplishments after school was out, happened to be an appointment at the Department of Motor Vehicles for both boys to take the written drivers license exam. They had been studying the manual for some time, but written tests are difficult for them. Bruce requested an oral exam, and they both came home with a driver's permit. They had both been driving around the farm for sometime, though entirely too cautiously. Allowing them behind the wheel on the road was a totally new ball game. I found myself freaking out more times than I want to admit. I couldn't remember being that scared when riding with our first three permit holders. One day, it hit us! Our three had been riding in cars since they were babies and had watched us drive all of their lives. Joseph and Paul had almost no experience with cars, whatsoever, before coming to America. No wonder, it was a bit more scary for me, and them as well! Thankfully, Bruce is a good driving instructor, and they are both becoming seasoned drivers. In fact, Joseph passed the road test on his first try, and Paul is soon to take his. I jokingly told my friends that being a Senior Citizen Soccer Mom is a piece of cake, but being a Senior Citizen Driving Instructor was about over the top for me!

Most of the summer was spent in summer school. Paul took Biology at Monte Vista to get caught up on some of his requirements. It turned out to be an intense six weeks for him. Thankfully, due to a bunch of hard work, he passed. He has one more requirement out of the way. The week following summer school, he helped—once again—at Kids Summer Adventure. He was an assistant to the game leader, Bill Campbell. He had much more fun this time playing with all of the children as they came through that station. Joseph decided to take an English class at Cabrillo College. We felt that this would give him a head start and allow him to become familiar with the campus before going full time in the fall. He got up early each morning on his own, and caught the bus at 6:40 am. at the bottom of our long driveway. He then transferred at the shopping center, and made it to his 8:00 class. He, too, passed his course.

School left little time for much activity, but we were able to squeeze in about a week for a trip to Spokane. Craig and three of his children joined us for part of the week. He had come to help install granite counter tops in two of the apartments we have there. Between Bruce, Craig, Andrew, and one of our boys each day, the job was accomplished in the first two days. The other boy would stay with me, and we would entertain Dominic and Kaitlin. It was fun to see them enjoy Riverfront Park and swimming in the motel pool. The third day, we all went to a lake so that the kids could fish. Joseph caught the biggest one, which we always call Walter. Craig started for home the next day. We drove on to Montana to meet up with sister, Kitty, and spend a few days at Glacier National Park. We all enjoyed seeing the splendor that is in such abundance there! The day after we arrived home, the boys were off to Soccer camp at Santa Clara University once again.

For many reasons, including high gas prices, Bruce and I decided to buy a new hybrid vehicle. The process was taking longer than expected, and I was led to believe that we wouldn't have the new car before leaving for Spokane. One evening, we were meeting some missionary friends for dinner. We all went out to the garage to get into the car. Much to my surprise, there was our brand new Toyota Highlander Hybrid! All three of my men had sheepish looks on their faces, because they had told me "little white lies" about what they had really been doing that afternoon. Needless to say, I was totally surprised! Bruce shared that Paul had been really concerned that they had "lied" to me regarding their whereabouts. He felt better about it when he saw the surprised, pleased look on my face and my obvious pleasure in their scheme. Paul learned a small lesson about the difference between dishonesty and surprises.

A few days later, Paul was back in school for the beginning of his Junior Year. Joseph still had a few weeks before his college classes started, so he worked hard with Bruce on the new sunroom/game room that we were building onto our home. Bruce's mom had noticed how much the boys enjoyed playing pool when we visited her. After his father died, she gave us his pool table. That motivated us to build this room. Since it has been finished, the boys have adopted this room as their own. At times we see them sprawled out on the soft carpet in the room, just soaking up the sun. That warm sun is a subtle reminder to them of the hot Sudanese sunshine that they had soaked up in their youth.

We had a special visitor for two weeks in August — our precious little grandson TJ. Tony and Lili went on a cruise with her mom and sister to celebrate her mom's birthday. We had the privilege of caring for him in their absence. When TJ was a baby, he took a strange dislike that stemmed from a fear of Joseph and Paul. It was quite clear that, with no outside motivation, this little baby understood that the boys' skin color was different, and in his little mind to be feared. This was in stark contrast to the relationship that Joseph and Paul had with every child they had encountered so far. When the boys would reach for him, he would cry. This was an embarrassment to Tony and Lili. One of the obvious benefits of having TJ stay with us for two weeks was for our grandson to develop a closer bond with us. We were also hopeful that he would develop a closer bond with Joseph and Paul. Over the next two weeks, this little guy grew so close to the boys, that at times he chose them over Bruce and I. If they went outside to work on their car, he was right there with them. He would stand at the door, so they would take him outside. One day, after his nap, he went looking for them. Paul was at school, and Joseph had gone somewhere. He searched for them, and came out of their room crying because they were nowhere to be found. He really loves Joseph and Paul, and they love him!

Reflections

Chapter 28

The educational process continues to be the biggest challenge we face. Having not had the opportunity to receive much education, indeed missing out entirely on junior high school, there is a tremendous void. So many concepts that American students are exposed to in their early years (and built upon in subsequent years) are just not in their frame of reference. The language barrier aside, how does a boy from a small African village understand things like "initiative, referendum and recall?"

It was just recently as we sat at the dinner table that they shared with us about attending the Islamic school in Sudan when they were young. As I sat and listened to them tell of the pressure and whippings, I could hardly hold back a tear. These special boys had stood up for their faith in Jesus and didn't waver! I couldn't help but wonder what I would have done at such a young age in their circumstances.

Despite the difficulty in this area of education, they are working diligently. We certainly believe that our Lord will bless their efforts.

The social scene continues to be a growing area

for the boys also. They really enjoy talking with people at church. Bruce and I like to hang around after the service to visit. Undoubtedly, when we're ready to leave, we find them still socializing.

Dating in America is so totally different from their culture. On one of those rare Saturday nights when our company left early, we four were sitting in the living room, just talking. They shared with us that in Sudan, if they liked a girl, they had to keep it between them and her only. Apparently, girls are in demand there. If other boys knew that you liked a girl, you would be beaten up. They literally fight over the girls! Their courting is very discreet, and when they want to marry, they go to her parents. Sometimes, cows are required for a dowry. If the parents agree, they are invited into the home to consummate the marriage. Soon after, there is a ceremony to make it public. For those in Christian villages, it involves a religious ceremony, and there is a celebration where the mothers of the bride and groom dance.

One evening at dinner during Joseph's first year, he was kind of chuckling to himself. I asked him what he was thinking about, and he told us that if he were still in Sudan, he would probably be married already. Of course, I asked him how he would support his wife and where they would live. He answered that they would live in his parents' home, and he would continue to help his dad with the cows. Eventually he and his wife would be able to build their own home. Joseph has readily agreed that he wants to marry someday, and he looks forward to having children. He jokingly says that he wants a wife who is Hispanic because he likes Mexican food! Paul is more reserved in discussions of marriage. At first, he said he didn't want to marry. However, of late, he says that he wants to go back to Africa to find a wife. They enjoy the company of girls, both African American girls, as well as white girls.

Another interesting twist in the life story of Joseph and Paul is that recently we met with a lady from the Red Cross. She is conducting a search for any known, living relatives of the boys. They actually wrote a message for her to include in the paper work. They wanted to let whoever may be found, their whereabouts and that they are well and being educated.

As part of the URM program, the boys are in the process of obtaining U.S. citizenship. This takes about five years. Of course, until citizenship is achieved, they do not have a passport. We wish they could travel on mission trips with us, but this will have to wait until they are well into the citizenship process. The URM program will continue to assist the boys until the age of 24, if certain requirements are met. When they are 19, they can choose to get help living on their own—as long as they are in school and have part-time jobs. Or, in Joseph's case (and Paul's as of January, 2009) they can choose to stay in their foster homes as long as they are in school. We are happy that they are both choosing to stay, and we are totally committed to helping them become educated, self-sufficient adults. If, in the future, they would like to get an apartment, we will help them get settled. We've told them both that we would like to take them back to the Sudan for a visit (or to stay, if they choose) after they graduate from college.

One day, our African friends from church invited us over to their home. They had an older car—a Nissan Sentra—sitting in their garage. They decided to give it to the boys, and signed over the pink slip to them on the spot. These two loyal friends are so eager to see the boys succeed! They sometimes help them with schoolwork, too. Bruce and I really appreciate the pep talks that they give to Joseph and Paul about working hard to succeed in this land of opportunity. They always encourage the boys to help us around the house and to be thankful. (I love it!)

Throughout these past three years, I have absolutely marveled at Bruce and the fantastic father he is to Paul and Joseph. His great love for them is so apparent. He handles them with such wisdom. He jokes and teases with them, but possesses that gentle firmness when necessary. My guys really have fun together! There is a closeness between them that allows Bruce to discuss any subject with them. We all got a huge chuckle out of an incident that happened while we were watching T.V. one night. We're always sensitive to the boys hearing something they might not understand, so it's not unusual for him to ask them if they understood what they heard and/or saw. On one particular occasion, the boys saw their first ad for "male enhancement pills". Toward the end of the ad, it occurred to Bruce that this was probably a new phenomenon to them.

Bruce looked over to Joseph, and just as he was about to ask if they understood that ad, he had an inquiring look on his face that gave us the answer. Joe said, "Is that talking about what I think it is?" Bruce confirmed that his concerns were accurate, and that there was actually medicine to help men that nature wasn't very kind to. An incredulous look appeared on his face, and the words, "Oh COME ON!" came out with equal shares of disgust and embarrassment. At other times, he'll look at us and say, "YOU'VE GOT TO BE KIDDING!"

Through his servant leadership style, Bruce has modeled and shown the boys that it is a positive thing to have a close relationship with their white mom. It has made a huge difference! It is now part of them to show gratitude for the things I do for them, and they treat me with much love and respect. They have grasped the way in which the American culture respects women.

From the Heart

Chapter 29

We are eagerly anticipating the future for Joseph and Paul. We have assured them that we will support their future efforts—whether in America or a return to Africa—after they are educated and have their citizenship. We firmly claim Jeremiah 29:11 for them: "For I know the plans I have for you," declares the Lord. "Plans to prosper you and not to harm you, plans to give you a hope and a future." Paul's dream is to, one day, return to his village to build a school and a hospital. We certainly encourage him and remind him that "all things are possible with the Lord!"

It has now been almost three years since Joseph and Paul have graced our home. The journey has had its share of rough spots. There have been times when we wondered if we had done the right thing. There were tears shed on our pillows at night, where more than once, we questioned whether we were up for this important task. Each challenge we were faced with, required a different solution. But as we look back, our Lord helped us with each one, sometimes in miraculous ways. In retrospect,

I would say that in fact, it was the challenges that have lent to the riches we have reaped these three years.

Our home has reverberated with laughter that we could have missed out on. Two young men have developed in ways they would have never had the opportunity to do. It is our conviction that the Lord will be served for generations to come because of the efforts these two wonderful young men will put into serving Him. To think that we struggled with a decision to move forward, shame on us! We are so thankful that we had taken that initial step of obedience. These precious young men have made an indelible mark on our hearts. We know that the Lord has a great plan for their lives, and we want to help them achieve their dreams.

Though the past three years have been—in many ways—a challenge for me, I can honestly say that I am exceedingly grateful for Joseph and Paul. They have blessed my life in so many ways! They now joke and tease with me, and are very thoughtful. These two young men are my heroes, and I tell them that quite often. It has been an amazing adventure! Someday, I hope to write a sequel about the things that they are able to accomplish in their lives. For now, I thank our dear Lord that, *though I was a stranger, they have invited me into their hearts!*

Information About the Unaccompanied Refugee Minor Program

The following information regarding the URM Program is taken from the web page of the U.S. Department of Health & Human Services — Office of Refugee Resettlement:

http://www.acf.hhs.gov/programs/orr/programs/unaccompanied_refugee_minors.htm

The State Department identifies refugee children overseas who are eligible for resettlement in the U.S., but do not have a parent or a relative available and committed to providing for their long term care. Upon arrival in the U.S., these refugee children are placed into the Unaccompanied Refugee Minors (URM) program and receive refugee foster care services and benefits.

The program was originally developed in the 1980s to address the needs of thousands of children in Southeast Asia without a parent or guardian to care for them. Since 1980, almost 12,000 minors have entered the URM program. At its peak in 1985, ORR provided protection to 3,828 children in care. Now in various States, ORR has about 600 children in care. While most children are placed in licensed foster homes, other licensed care settings are utilized according to children's individual needs, such as therapeutic foster care, group homes, residential treatment centers, and independent living programs.

Children eligible for the URM Program are under age 18, are unaccompanied and are:

- Refugees
- Entrants
- Asylees
- Victims of Trafficking

Two lead voluntary agencies—Lutheran Immigration Refugee Service (LIRS) and the United States Conference of Catholic Bishops (USCCB)—help ORR with the unaccompanied refugee minor program.

Geographic Locations: Phoenix, AZ; San Jose, CA; Washington, DC; Miami, FL; Boston/Worcester, MA; Lansing, MI; Grand Rapids, MI; Jackson, MS; Fargo, ND; Rochester, NY; Syracuse, NY; Philadelphia, PA; Sioux Falls, SD; Dallas, TX; Houston, TX; Salt Lake City, UT; Richmond, VA; Tacoma, WA; Seattle, WA.

Additional information can be obtained at:

- www.usccb.org/mrs/urmdesc.shtml
- www.lirs.org/InfoRes/faq/fostercare.htm

Being a foster parent to an unaccompanied refugee minor is truly a rewarding experience. We highly recommend it!